LYFTING
LA

LYFTING LA

NINE YEARS BEFORE THE DASH

L. A. CARSTENS

Lyfting LA
Copyright © 2025 by L. A. Carstens
All rights reserved.

This is a work of fiction. Names, characters, organizations, places, events and incidents are either the products of the author's imagination or are used fictitiously. Any resemblance to actual persons, living or dead, or actual events is purely coincidental.

Editing, design, and distribution by Bublish

ISBN: 978-1-64704-960-7 (eBook)
ISBN: 978-1-64704-962-1 (Paperback)

How many goodly creatures are there here!
How beauteous mankind is! O brave new world,
That has such people in't.

—William Shakespeare

CONTENTS

PREFACE

Somewhere around the beginning of 2016, the car I was driving died. The timing belt broke while I was on Interstate 5, and the engine expired, never to recover. I still owed a few thousand dollars on it, and the cost of repairing it exceeded its value. It was time to get another car. I wanted something reliable and economic—a Toyota Prius—but I knew a brand-new one was beyond my budget. So I would get a used one. But how would I afford that?

I decided to drive for Lyft. With all my other commitments, I wasn't sure when I would be able to find the time, but I would try to do it a few nights per week, and so the car would hopefully pay for itself.

Before I started, I had fears and misgivings about what I was about to do. I had listened to horror stories of what could go wrong, from people who knew people who used to do it and quit. I was told that I would have to give rides to drunk people who would throw up in my car, that I would destroy my car with all the miles I would put on it, and that I might get robbed or beaten up. None of those things happened—except the part about giving rides to drunk people, but they were nice to me, at least most of the time. And although I have put a lot of miles on my car, the income has helped to counterbalance the expenses enough to make it worth it.

I didn't realize how much I would enjoy driving for Lyft. The conversations are probably the most interesting thing about it. Not everybody wants to talk, and I respect those who don't, but a lot of them do, and what they tell me is something of an education in itself, like reading a wide variety of books by a wide variety of authors. And so, as an English teacher who loves reading and who fancies himself a writer, I decided to tell some of their stories, keeping most of the identities anonymous, since I didn't ask their permission, but describing the details I found interesting, funny, instructive, or otherwise noteworthy.

As I was working on this, I realized that my past experiences as a local history nerd—visiting sites of historic and aesthetic interest—enriched my conversations with passengers and might also enrich this presentation of stories, so the focus would be of a dual nature: on LA's past and its present. These stories describe the people who started and built up Los Angeles and the people who ride its streets today.

About the subtitle: *Nine Years before the Dash* is a kind of allusion to *Two Years before the Mast*, which was one of the earliest accounts of travels along the California coast of the 1830s—when it was still territory of Mexico—by the Yankee writer Richard Henry Dana. This book played a significant role in the development of California into an American territory and later a state, since its publication resulted in significant public interest in the California coast during the period leading up to the Mexican-American War and the transfer of California from Mexican to American territory. One part of the California coast, Dana Point, is named in honor of its author.

About the title: *Lyfting LA* means what it looks like. It's a description of experiences while driving for Lyft around the greater metropolitan area of Los Angeles, my home for most of my five (now almost six) decades of life.

But the title also works on another level. The first two initials of my real birth name (it's not a pseudonym or a pen name) are L. A., which stands for Larry Alan. I'm not sure why my parents chose the name Larry, but my mother had an admiration for an actor named Alan Ladd, and that's the basis for my middle name. Growing up, I never saw any of Alan Ladd's films, but I did have a teenager's admiration for his daughter-in-law, actress Cheryl Ladd . . . for her acting ability, of course. I rather doubt that my parents intended my first two initials to be identical to the city where I would spend most of my life, but it happened that way, and now I can refer to myself as Lyfting LA.

What this means is that the pages that follow flow from my experience as a part-time Lyft driver in Los Angeles. Other drivers may have other encounters and other thoughts. These are mine. I am Lyfting LA.

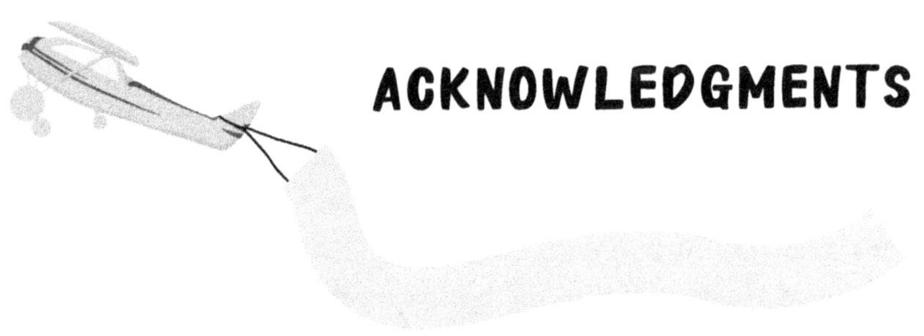

ACKNOWLEDGMENTS

There are always people who deserve recognition and thanks whenever a book is written, and this one is no exception. I am grateful to the ten-thousand-plus passengers who have allowed me to drive them to their destinations, even the ones who didn't wish to have a conversation. If you read this and recognize that you were my passenger, you're always welcome to send an email to *lyftinglawriter@gmail.com* to say hello. If you *did* have a conversation with me, and if you recognize it here, please let me know if I got anything wrong or missed any important details.

I am grateful to all the people who took the time to look over drafts of parts of this book and offer helpful feedback: my dad, Ed Carstens; my stepmom, Elaine Madsen Carstens; my brothers, Brian, Bruce, Ken, and Doug Carstens; my friends and fellow educators, Ethel Matlen and Dr. James Hanink; and anyone else who offered encouragement and/or criticism. I am grateful to my colleagues and fellow local history nerds, Eric Grow and John Wood; to all the teachers of the Los Angeles Unified School District (LAUSD) who have taken our classes focusing on the history and culture of the greater Los Angeles area; and to all the wonderful docents, like Christian Hernandez (at the Lummis House) and Rita Bazeley (at the Gamble House, which was the abode of Dr. Emmet Brown in the *Back to the Future* trilogy), who guided us through many amazing experiences of the places and people who shaped LA. I am grateful to the Los Angeles Conservancy, which has fought to preserve a significant number of historic buildings. Their members have also led my colleagues and me on wonderful walking tours of the city that is our home.

And I am grateful to the honest mechanic, Sargon Karamian, whose expertise and trustworthiness has kept my Lyft mobile on the road. I've enjoyed our philosophical conversations and have appreciated his encouragement of this project and the times he would ask, "So how's your book coming along?"

Lastly, I am grateful to God, whose grace has allowed me the experiences and the ability to get this done. Ad majorem Dei gloriam.

1

MY DAY JOB

And I have found that nothing is better than for a man to rejoice in his work, and that this is his portion.

—Ecclesiastes 3:22

IN THE YEARS I've been driving for Lyft, one thing I've learned from listening to my passengers is that there are all kinds of other people who do it as a side hustle. I've heard about college students, professors, and even a church pastor who do it. Once, a gentleman from a nice suburb told me how he recently had to take a Lyft from his home to LAX at the same time in the morning, several mornings in a row. He noticed that the same driver was picking him up each time, and so he asked him about it. It turned out the driver was a medical doctor whose hospital was not far from LAX, so he would accept ride requests from people who were going in that direction at that time of the morning, and it just happened that the passenger was doing just that, at the same time on multiple mornings. So it would seem that I've become part of a community of educated professionals who do Lyft on the side to supplement their income.

I first became a Lyft driver in January 2016. But I continued with my day job, which was as a high school English teacher for LAUSD. That was, and still is, my full-time job—the main means of income that has enabled me to support a wife and five children and to pay a mortgage in Southern California as well as all the other bills and taxes that go with those things. It is also my source of medical coverage and a retirement plan. One thing about working as a teacher is that a lot of financial issues are predictable through the years, which is a good source of peace of mind. But the downside is the knowledge that you'll never get rich. You have a steady and predictable income, and you don't experience a lot of the uncertainty that goes with other lines of work, but you also know that the position will never pay millions, the way becoming a star can in sports, entertainment, the media, or corporate America.

Although I have a comfortable income and the bases of life are covered, I've always been interested in ways to supplement my wages. Sixteen years ago, I earned a master's degree in English and started working part time at a community college. Around that time, I also earned National Board Certification, which adds about 12 to 15 percent to my annual pay, and I started teaching professional development classes for teachers on Saturdays. Then I began driving for Lyft.

I had no idea how much I would actually enjoy it. I was prepared to do it even if I didn't like it, but the fact that I did was a pleasant surprise. What makes it so enjoyable? I'd have to say the interesting people and conversations, not with every single passenger, of course, but with a significant percentage; it's enough so that it stays interesting. There's also the feeling that you're helping people; you're providing a service that seems simple but means a lot—a clean, safe ride from point A to point B in a massive, sometimes dangerous, and sometimes unfriendly city. I especially feel a sense of community service when I do something that I was warned about when I first discussed the idea with friends and family. But it has turned out to be not so bad after all, giving rides home late at night to people who are too drunk or too stoned to drive themselves. The drunk or stoned people who I have Lyfted home have never been unpleasant with me, though I must admit I wouldn't want to be their roommate or spouse, and they have never fouled my car's interior. I have heard stories that it happens, and I'm sure it does, but it hasn't happened to *me* (out of more than ten thousand rides and counting!). So I enjoy it, and I like the sort of street smarts education I get by listening to my passengers talk about whatever is on their minds. I learn about how sports teams are doing after I Lyft people near Dodger Stadium, the Staples Center, or the Coliseum; I learn about some of the hottest concerts when I talk to fans leaving the Hollywood Bowl, the Forum, or the cutting-edge comedy or concert clubs on Sunset Strip or just off Hollywood Boulevard. I also talk to people from all over the world who are tourists in LA: people from England, France, Germany, Russia, Brazil, Korea, China, the Philippines, and, even a few times, from Africa or the Middle East.

As I talk with my passengers and ask them about their day, the conversation often leads to them asking about my day. If it's in the evening, my morning and early afternoon were typically spent in a classroom, so often I respond, "It's fine! Driving for Lyft is easy. My day job is more of a challenge." Then they usually ask about the day job, and I tell them I'm a teacher, and then they almost always say something like "That's great," or "Thanks so much for what you do." Occasionally, they say something like "My hat is off to you. I could *never* do something like that." Sometimes they get indignant or even a bit angry—not at me but at the system in which someone who is an intelligent guy (I'm just quoting them) with a master's degree has to drive for Lyft to make ends meet. When someone says that, I respond that I don't feel as if I *have* to drive for Lyft but it's a good side gig that's fun and helps pay the bills. Of course, I heartily agree with them when they say that teachers should be paid much, much more than they currently are for the work they do!

Sometimes I compare driving for Lyft with teaching high school in a way that makes them chuckle. When I drive, I don't have to argue with anyone about where they're going or convince them why they should go there. I don't have to try to control anyone's behavior or try to explain why they shouldn't act like a fool in my classroom. I don't have to threaten or punish people who don't want to go where I'm taking them; everyone I deal with wants to be there and knows why they're doing what they're doing. They want my help, and they're glad when I assist them. When teaching high school, a teacher has to be against their students in some ways, or the students take advantage and walk all over them. Even when students like you as their teacher, there's still a sense that you and they are on opposite sides, and they still try to avoid doing work or respecting the rules of your class. Driving for Lyft is still work, but after teaching high school, it's almost like it's not work. Another aspect of it is that I can quit for the evening whenever I feel like it.

Teaching college is less stressful, and a college instructor can generally do more actual educating and a lot less behavior management, but there's still some degree of pressure and hard work that goes into planning lessons and grading papers at the college level. The actual teaching that happens in a college class is much more enjoyable to me. The students are more mature and understand many of my jokes, and they get it and listen more attentively when I'm talking about what they need to do to complete assignments and succeed in my class. But it still has its own kind of stress or pressure, which is wholly absent from Lyft driving.

My third teaching job is also part time and involves organizing and leading professional development classes for teachers of LAUSD. One aspect of this kind of class involves participants visiting and writing about local sites of cultural or historic interest in the greater Los Angeles area. This has been interesting and enjoyable work, too, and it has contributed to my work as a Lyft driver. In the fifteen years I have done this, I have learned a great deal about the local history and lore of places in and around Los Angeles. It makes for interesting conversation when I pick up passengers at, or drive past, sites that are important in the history of Los Angeles. For example, Union Station was the last of the great city train stations to be built; all the major cities back east already had theirs.

Union Station, Los Angeles, the last of the major city train stations.

Union Station in Los Angeles was completed in 1939, just as cars and airplanes were becoming the main means for long trips between large cities. Just about five hundred feet in front of Union Station is Olvera Street Plaza, the site where forty-four people arrived in 1776 on a charter from the king of Spain and established the little settlement called El Pueblo de la Reyna de Los Angeles (the name was shortened to Los Angeles after the Americans took California in 1848). Those forty-four souls who founded Los Angeles, probably with no idea that their little settlement would grow to become the second largest city in North America, did so in the same year that some troublemaking colonists from Britain were declaring their independence from King George III and starting a new country on the East Coast.

My son James stands in front of the statue of the king of Spain, whose charter led to the founding of Los Angeles. Union Station is visible in the background.

If I drive by the corner of Wilshire and Western, I sometimes mention to passengers that it was one of the first intersections with an automated traffic light in Los Angeles and how the famed Wiltern Theatre at the same intersection was named by merging the names of the two streets that meet there. Sometimes I tell passengers how the stretch of the 110 Freeway between downtown and Pasadena (a.k.a. the Arroyo Seco Parkway) is the oldest freeway in the city, which explains why the curves, on-ramps, and off-ramps are more intense than most other freeways that were built later, when the people constructing them realized that cars would be traveling at much higher speeds than they did in the 1920s and 1930s. Sometimes I recommend museums like the Getty Center, the Getty Villa, the Huntington, or the Los Angeles County Museum of Art (LACMA), all of which I have visited with groups of teachers as part of the classes I organize.

And so my day job and my part-time jobs all seem to work together: My teaching jobs enrich and enliven my role as a driver and an ad hoc tour guide for my passengers around the streets and sites of Los Angeles. I usually, but not always, get five-star ratings from them, along with comments like "Best Lyft driver ever!" and "Thanks for an interesting conversation!" Even though I've always given my passengers five-star ratings, I have occasionally received less than five stars or a critical comment. What's particularly disconcerting is when I get a low rating because the navigation system misled me, for example, to a back alley when the passenger wanted to be picked up or dropped off in front. Somehow they consider that my fault when it obviously wasn't. One other comment I received probably came from someone who put a bag in the back of my car, which is usually cluttered with books and/or papers from one of my teaching jobs. I typically keep the front and back passenger sections fairly clean, and most people never see the trunk, but occasionally, when they have luggage or a lot of shopping bags, they do see it. The comment said, "He could clean his car." I have to plead guilty to that one, but I also added (in my mind), *Let's see* you *try to juggle all these jobs and have a perfect car every day!*

My fifth job (fourth part-time job, actually) is as an author. I write books. They don't become bestsellers, but they entertain friends and family. Perhaps this one is entertaining you!

2

RITA HAYWORTH AND THE DRAW-BLANK CONFESSION

Rita Hayworth hung in Andy's cell until 1955, if I remember right. Then it was Marilyn Monroe.

—Stephen King,
Rita Hayworth and the Shawshank Redemption

Somewhere in the heart of Hollywood, near the intersection of Santa Monica and Highland, there's a high-culture music school. I don't recall the name of the school, but when I picked up a young man with a high-culture look, he told me about it. I remember thinking that it sounded a lot like the famed Julliard School in the Lincoln Center of the Performing Arts in New York City. The young man had semi-long but neatly cut hair, wore a classy (sort of) dinner jacket, and was carrying something that just radiated high culture—I think it may have been a cello or violin case.

We drove for a few blocks, then turned a corner onto Hayworth Avenue. As we did so, I said to him, "I wonder if they named this street after Rita Hayworth." I suppose I was thinking that this was a highly cultured young man who would know about Hollywood lore and the legends of Tinsel Town. I was wrong.

He responded, "Who's Rita Hayworth?"

"Well," I said, "she was a Hollywood movie star from the thirties and forties." She was kind of like the Angelina Jolie of her day. She was also a popular pinup girl during World War II. They made a lot of posters of her that the soldiers of that era used to put on their walls.

This is the iconic poster of Rita Hayworth that adorned countless walls and lockers of servicemen during World War II. It was probably the one Steven King had in mind when he penned Rita Hayworth and the Shawshank Redemption.

"Oh," he responded. We talked for a few minutes more, then we reached his destination. I dropped him off, wished him a good day, and gave him a five-star rating. He was still a very nice young man, even if he didn't know as much as I thought he would.

Every ride on the Lyft app asks the user to rate the passenger at the end of the ride. I have always rated my passengers five stars. If anyone was rude or unpleasant, I wouldn't give them five stars, but I can honestly say that every one of the more than ten thousand passengers I have delivered to their destinations has been pleasant and cordial to deal with—or if not, at least neutral and quiet. Lines from Shakespeare's *Julius Caesar* come to mind. Just before he ends his own life, Marcus Brutus says, "My heart doth joy that in all my life / I found no man but he was true to me." The irony is that, as the audience knows, Brutus's close friend and coconspirator against Caesar (Cassius) was deceiving Brutus from the beginning of the play to get him to turn against Caesar. But I don't think any of my passengers were attempting to do anything like that to *me*! And even though they almost always rode in the back seat, I never feared that they would pull a Julius Caesar on me and make me look in the rearview mirror and ask, "Et tu, Bruté?" No way, man. All my passengers were good people, and they always had my back—at least, it seemed that way to me.

After dropping off the young man, I remember thinking how strange it was that he hadn't heard of Rita Hayworth. She had always seemed to me like one of those people everyone knew about. Those of my parents' generation all knew who she was. Her name was even mentioned in the title of the 1982 Stephen King novella, *Rita Hayworth and the Shawshank Redemption*, which was later adapted for the big screen as the hit movie *The Shawshank Redemption*. But when they adapted it for film, Ms. Hayworth's name was cut out. In the novella, Stephen King used the poster of Rita Hayworth to indicate the passage of many years, actually decades. Early in the story, after the protagonist, Andy Dufresne, is framed and wrongfully imprisoned for the murder of his wife and her lover, he puts a poster of Rita Hayworth on the wall of his cell. As the years go by, he pins up posters of Marilyn Monroe (pinup girl of the 1950s) and Raquel Welch (pinup girl of the 1960s) on the same spot on his wall. When he finally escapes, the prison warden finds a poster of Linda Ronstadt (pinup girl of the 1970s) on his wall, and behind the poster is a hole in the wall, exposing a tunnel that he had been working on during all the intervening years.

So Rita Hayworth was an important part of the original Stephen King novella, even if she didn't get any mention in the motion picture. I thought her name was still a household word, even among the younger generation.

Anyway, a few weeks later, I picked up somebody closer to my own age in the same area—the heart of Hollywood, probably near Melrose, Santa Monica, or Sunset Boulevard. I talked with the older gentleman with the ease and comfort of someone from my own generation—you know, another person born in the 1960s, old enough to remember the hippies but too young to say, "You shoulda been at Woodstock!" I told him about the young man I had picked up a few weeks before. "When I turned the corner onto Hayworth Avenue, I said that I wondered if the street was named after Rita Hayworth. And he said to me, 'Who's Rita Hayworth?'" We both had a hearty laugh. Then there was a moment of silence as we continued to his destination. I didn't say anything, but my thoughts were along the lines of, *Kids these days. They don't even know who Rita Hayworth is.* I figured that my passenger was thinking along similar lines.

I was about to say something about the difference between our generation and millennials, but at that moment, we arrived at his destination. I slowed the car and pulled over. "Well, it's been nice talking with you," I said to the gentleman.

"You, too," he said cheerfully. As he reached for the door, he paused and turned to me thoughtfully, then asked a totally unexpected question: "So who *is* Rita Hayworth?"

3
PASSENGERS MISJUDGED

All the world's a stage, / and all the men and women merely players.

—William Shakespeare

EVERY SO OFTEN, first impressions are completely wrong. Sometimes passengers seem very nice at first, then turn out to be sourpusses. Other times, the opposite happens, and people I feared at first turn out to be really sweet and likeable.

One of the clearest examples of the latter happened when I picked up four really big, tattoo-covered football players late one night in Northridge. Sometimes when I pull up at a home where a party is happening, there are clumps of people standing (or stumbling around) outside, and I sort of secretly hope, *Not these guys. I hope they're not the ones who requested the ride.* When I picked up the four football players, my thoughts were along those lines. The first guy to get into my car told me that there would be three more coming and that they were good guys—or words to that effect. I recall thinking, *Yeah, right.*

As the other big guys got into the car, I remember feeling my little Prius C sink closer to the road. I also remember the sound of laughter and the smell of whiskey. Their large bodies barely fit into the seats of my little car. As I stepped down on the accelerator, it seemed like the car was more sluggish about moving forward. One of the four guys said, "You got about one thousand pounds of weight in your car right now, brah!"

Another one laughed and said, "Maybe we should take *two* Ubers!" At some point, I stopped correcting passengers who refer to a Lyft ride as an Uber.

One of the other passengers responded, "Nah, we fit in this car, brah! It's only a few miles to Steggy's house." Laughter followed.

At first, I thought they were using the Hawaiian term *brah* to try to sound cool. But I soon realized that they were actually *from* Hawaii. They spoke about friends, women, and football. As I listened to them and infrequently joined in the conversation, I realized that they were really sweet and accommodating—sort of gentle giants. I asked them about football, about their experiences in school (they played for a college football team), and about Hawaii. People love to talk about themselves; one key to success as a Lyft driver is to invite people to talk about who they are and what they do (as long as you recognize and respect the *other* type of passenger who prefers to be left alone).

The young man who sat next to me turned out to be especially nice and pleasant to converse with. Soon after I found out he was from Hawaii, I mentioned to him that my wife and kids had recently seen *Moana*, which was based on Hawaiian (animist) mythology. He said, "Yah, mon, that's a really good film, brah! It's the first movie to show our culture. They never paid much attention to our culture until now. Finally, now, they payin' attention to us!"

I said it was good that Disney was finally recognizing Hawaiian culture, but I wondered if they were presenting it with integrity or changing the story to the point where the original was almost impossible to recognize. I may have mentioned Disney classics such as *The Little Mermaid* and *Hercules*, which were enjoyable cartoons in their own right but substantially changed from the original stories. The original *Little Mermaid* (by Hans Christian Andersen) was a much darker story, ending with the death of the title character. The character in *Hercules* was enjoyable, as was the Hades bad guy character voiced by James Woods, but it was completely different from the portrayals of Hercules in the original stories of ancient Greek mythology.

I asked the genial young man who mentioned that he had seen *Moana* if he thought it misrepresented Hawaiian culture or mythology. Either he didn't understand my question or he didn't have an opinion on the matter. Perhaps he wasn't very knowledgeable of the original stories upon which *Moana* was based. He only replied, "It's a good film, mon. It shows our culture. You should see it, brah!"

When it came time to drop off my Hawaiian football player passengers, I was a little sad. When you think you're going to dread people whom you actually end up liking, it's kind of a downer to say goodbye. But it was said, then it was on to the next ride.

*　　*　　*

A few weeks later, I answered a request from two young women who emerged from a building a half block away from Hollywood and Highland. Their attractive attire suggested they were going out to a nightclub or bar. Their destination was in Koreatown, which would take about fifteen or twenty minutes to reach.

As we talked, they mentioned they were from New York, something I had guessed from their accents. They had recently driven into town from San Francisco and were planning to drive to San Diego the following day. I supposed that they were on a road trip adventure of some kind all around the country. They asked me questions about LA, which I was happy to answer. I mentioned that LA is second only to their hometown of New York in terms of population. They said there was a similar feel to the streets of LA, but some things were really different, specifically the lack of an extensive subway system that could be used to reach almost anywhere in the city, like they had in New York. I told them a bit about the history of LA—how it was little more than a small town for the first one hundred years of its existence (1781–1881). It sort of exploded into a metropolis during its second hundred years, and it didn't seem to plan out its expansion in any organized fashion. Places like San Francisco and New York (and London and Paris for that matter) had a lot more time to grow and develop as major cities. Los Angeles didn't really have that luxury; it just sort of boomed into the big city it is today because of the railroads, the oil industry, and then the entertainment and aerospace industries.

As I talked, the two young women seemed as if they were really enjoying the conversation. It was almost like the pleasure of teaching, when students really want to learn, not just because they have to but because they want to. I thought I was really helping to enlighten them on the subject of Los Angeles and its legacy. And perhaps I was, but when it was time to drop them off, something happened that caused me to doubt the effectiveness of my discourse on the wonders of Los Angeles.

As they were about to get out, there was a nervous giggle, and I heard one of them whisper to the other, "Who cares? It doesn't matter . . . just ask him!"

After taking a moment to summon her courage, the bolder one said, "I hope it doesn't offend you, but there's one more thing we wanted to ask you because we're not from here, you know?"

I said, "Sure. Ask away!" For a moment, I wondered what they would want to know about. The founding of LA, perhaps? The arrival of the Americans to California after 1848? The growth of the entertainment industry? Some interesting museums?

Then she asked, "Do you know where we can buy some marijuana?"

For a moment, I stumbled for an answer. "Sorry. I don't really know about that. I'm sort of an old-fashioned Mr. Rogers kind of guy. I'm really not into that."

"Okay, Mr. Rogers," one of them replied and giggled. "Well, if you were going to look for something like that in this town, where would you start?"

I said, "Now that it's legal, I would think there are dispensaries around." I thought for a moment. "I guess I would just use my phone and do a search for nearby places using the word *marijuana*." They laughed and thanked me, then walked across the street to their destination, which appeared to be some kind of nightclub in Koreatown.

I remember feeling strange and out of sorts. I never imagined that, in all the years I taught high school and all the times I warned students about alcohol, drugs, and marijuana, I would be giving two young women advice about where they might be able to get some.

But I suppose you never know where you'll be asked to go when you're driving for Uber—I mean, Lyft.

*　　*　　*

One of the most dramatic examples of a passenger I completely misjudged happened just after I dropped someone off in a rough area of South Central Los Angeles. Some Lyft drivers tap the Last

Ride option when they drop someone off in a rough neighborhood so that they won't get another request in the same area. I usually don't. Even in a rough neighborhood, people who have an active Lyft account are generally not the ones who would be a danger to a driver. Of course, there are rare incidents that end up in the news, but it's still highly unlikely that anyone would harm me, even if I pick them up in a not-so-great area.

There was one occasion in which I wondered if I might be in some danger. It happened like this: I had just dropped off a passenger in South Central LA and received a request from another person. We'll call him Dante. This was not his real name, but it's sometimes heard in South LA neighborhoods, and it also happens to be the name of one of the greatest Renaissance poets (the guy who wrote the *Inferno* and the rest of the *Divina Commedia* in the early 1300s, but I digress).

I stopped in front of the apartment building where I was supposed to pick up Dante. Soon after, I saw a policeman leading a young Black man in handcuffs toward the street, where a black-and-white SUV was parked. They were heading toward me, but I fully expected them to pass by and get in the police vehicle. Instead, the handcuffed young man looked over at me and told the cop, "That's my Uber!"

I started to get increasingly uncomfortable as the cop led the young man toward my car, and he leaned down as if to tell me something. I lowered my window, and he said, "Just give me a couple of minutes. You're here for Dante, right?" I nodded, and then he said, "That's me. Don't leave. I'll be right back."

At this point I had been driving for Lyft for more than six years, and I had never had someone in handcuffs tell me not to leave. I wasn't sure if I was going to wait, but then the cop confirmed what the young man in handcuffs had said: "Yeah, he'll be right out in a couple of minutes. This won't take very long." Then he led

Dante back into the building. Sure enough, about two minutes later, Dante reappeared without the handcuffs on and without the cop. He got into my car, and we started off.

After I drove for a couple of blocks, my curiosity got the best of me. "I hope you don't mind my asking, but what happened back there?"

He replied, "Yeah, I guess it looked pretty crazy, huh?"

"Yeah, it did."

"It's cool. I don't mind telling you what happened," he said. "I was just trying to see this girl who I really love, and things got bad. We started yelling at each other, and she called the cops on me and told them I was abusing her. They came right away, but they could tell she was just trying to get me in trouble. Even her sister told the cops I wasn't abusing her. I'm not that kind of guy."

"That's why the cop told me to wait for you."

"That's right."

"So you're not a bad guy at all."

"No, sir. I was the best thing that happened to that girl, and she even told me so, before everything got all messed up."

"It sounds like you and she had a good thing going on for a while, huh?"

"Yeah. She was living on the street when I first got to know her. She had been in an abusive relationship before that. I helped her to rebuild her life and get back on her feet. She even told me how she felt so much better about herself and everything because of me."

"But things have changed since then?"

"She changed. She told me she doesn't feel the same way about me now," he said sadly. "I still feel the same about her. She's the only girl I've ever really loved like this."

"Mind if I ask how old you are?"

"It's cool, bro. I'm twenty years old. I'll be twenty-one next summer."

"Oh, so you're still young. You might have other relationships in the future. I know you must have heard this before, but there are a lot of young women out there."

"Not like this one," he said. "And the time I spent with her, building her up and helping her to live again—I don't think I can ever have that again with anyone else."

"I know this might seem hard for you to believe," I said, trying to act like the best love doctor I could, "but you might meet somebody else, and you might build up something even deeper and more meaningful."

"But I just can't see myself with anyone else. And I know she really loved me before . . ." His voice broke, and he started to cry. I remember thinking how this tough-looking guy I had first seen in handcuffs was really just a shaken-up young man who was unlucky in love.

"Well," I told him, "maybe she did have feelings for you in the past, but whatever you had, as wonderful as it was, it's over. I'm not a professional therapist or anything, but in my opinion, it's time for you to move on."

"I know," he said between sniffles. "I got to face the facts. But it's hard, because I loved her so much. I still love her! I wish I didn't . . ."

There was a pause. I'd had the radio on and a song was playing, "Save Your Tears" by the Weeknd.

"Could you please change that?" he asked.

"What, you mean the song?"

"Yeah. I don't want to hear that song right now."

"Okay," I said. I changed the radio to another station.

"Thanks, man," he said. "That was like her favorite song. I'm just not ready to listen to it right now."

"I understand. I know how it is when you associate a song with a past relationship that becomes a painful memory."

"But I didn't want this to be a past relationship. That's why I went to see her—to try to make things work again."

"Okay, but *she* didn't want to make things work again, and she even called the cops on you. I think that means you need to move on."

He didn't respond, and soon we arrived at his destination. "Here's my stop, bro," he said. "Thanks for listening to me and all my problems."

"No problem. I've been through similar experiences," I said as he opened the door. "I hope you find another person who's better for you."

"I don't know," he said, "but it was good talking with you."

"You, too," I responded. "Hang in there. Things will get better. You'll see."

"Thanks, man. Drive safe." He got out and closed the door.

I don't know where Dante is now, but I sure hope he's with someone who loves him. He was a sweet guy, and he deserves a sweet girl.

As I drove away, the Police song "Message in a Bottle" played in my mind.

4

I'VE LIVED ALL OVER THIS TOWN

Los Angeles is a true postmodern city. Here, we celebrate with equal aplomb the high and the low.

—Liz Goldwyn

WHEN I CONVERSE with local passengers, we sometimes talk about places we've lived and worked. People from East LA like it when I mention that I once lived in Montebello and another time in Boyle Heights. I form a special bond with those from the South Bay, since that's where I grew up, in the part of Torrance that's close to Redondo Beach. I relate with residents of the San Fernando Valley, since that's where I've worked for most of my teaching career. My residence has been in Castaic, right next to Santa Clarita and Magic Mountain, for most of my adult life.

I still remember specific aspects of the first time I entered the LA area. It was 1972, and I was seven years old, riding in the back of my parents' Country Squire station wagon, along with my four brothers. Our first stop was a Chinese restaurant called Louie's Chinese Garden on Pacific Coast Highway (probably in Lomita or Harbor City). We had left from Chapel Woods, Missouri, a few days earlier. Before that, we lived in Jeddah, Saudi Arabia, for two years. And before *that*, we lived in Kansas and Nebraska, the state where I was born in a small town called Hebron. All these places figure into the conversation when I learn that passengers are from the places I have been. When I talk with people from the Midwest, I tell them about the small town in Nebraska where I was born. When I speak with people from the Middle East, I mention my experience for two years as a child in Saudi Arabia. I have similar connections with people from the United Kingdom, where I lived as a college student for a semester; from Spain, where I worked for a year as a teacher; and from France or the Philippines, where I visited loved ones multiple times.

After living for seven years in Torrance, I went to stay at a Catholic minor (high school) seminary in Montebello, which was my principal residence for two and a half years. I lived in a dormitory at the school but came home on some weekends and during the summer. After I was expelled from the seminary, for reasons I prefer not to go into here (though I will mention that it happened not too long after I told the dean of students, who was also a priest, to go to hell), I returned to Torrance and lived there for most of the 1980s. I finished high school there, then took a year off from formal education and began surfing. After that, I attended El Camino College in Torrance. After saving up money from delivering for Domino's Pizza, I studied abroad in Cambridge, England, for a semester, then finished my bachelor's degree at Loyola Marymount University, where I lived on campus for two years.

During this time, my views about LA underwent an evolution of their own. If you had asked me when I was an adolescent and a young adult if I liked Los Angeles, I would have responded, "No way, man! There are too many things wrong with this town." Teenagers are known for their cynical and critical attitudes, and I was no different. I saw LA as a sort of web of superficiality and deception. I heartily agreed with the cynical assessment of the Hollywood dream factory in Nathanael West's classic 1939 novel, *The Day of the Locust* (which borrowed imagery from Kevin Whale's 1931 film adaptation of Mary Shelley's *Frankenstein* in its characterization of Homer Simpson, whose name would later be used by Matt Groenig, the creator of *The Simpsons*). In West's novel, Hollywood was a sort of nightmare of disordered desires, where people came from all over the county seeking fame and fortune, only to be disappointed. Because it's so ironic and darkly funny, one of my favorite descriptions in *The Day of the Locust* is found in chapter 1. As the main character walks near Vine Street,

> [He] examined the evening crowd. A great many of the people wore sports clothes which were not really sports clothes. Their sweaters, knickers, slacks, blue flannel jackets with brass buttons were fancy dress. The fat lady in the yachting cap was going shopping, not boating; the man in the Norfolk jacket and Tyrolean hat was returning, not from a mountain, but an insurance office; and the girl in slacks and sneaks with a bandanna around her head had just left a switchboard, not a tennis court.

Growing up as a young man in the Los Angeles area, I also saw the drug culture up close, the sleazy nightclubs and the porn industry, and all the shattered lives and broken dreams of people who had come here hoping to make it big but failing to achieve their dreams. So in the days of my youth, my answer to "Do you like LA?" would have been a resounding no. Besides cynicism, another aspect for youth is idealism, and my youthful idealism led me to try to make things better.

One of the first things I did after graduating from college in 1989 was volunteer at a soup kitchen on Skid Row. For two months I lived with the community (the Catholic Worker) and helped serve hundreds of homeless people a few days a week. After I had befriended one of the men we were serving, I took him up on his invitation to hang out with him and his friends. I remember sitting around a fire with them on wooden crates set out on a sidewalk in Skid Row, the area of downtown where most homeless people can be found. There were about seven of us, and I was the only one who was not African American. I don't remember exactly what we were talking about, but I remember feeling safe and welcome. They didn't mind speaking with me; it was as if we were old friends.

As we were talking, they had some dinner, which was food given to them at the back of a Japanese restaurant, then they took out some crack pipes. They offered me some, but when I declined, they didn't seem to mind. Suddenly, one of them said, "Cops!" and they all put their crack pipes away.

A few moments later, a police car pulled up in front of us. It was dark, so the cop turned on his sidecar searchlight and focused it on each one of us. I saw the light go from one of my companions to another, in succession, from right to left. I was probably the fifth person from the cop's right. The light went on me, then to the man sitting next to me. Then it came back to me. The cop asked, "Who's he?"

My host replied, "Oh, he's just my friend. He hangin' out wid us fo a while." A moment later, the squad car rumbled off. Later that evening, my friend arranged some cardboard for me, and I spent the night on the sidewalk, right there in the heart of Skid Row, not far from the corner of Seventh and Gladys. It was surprisingly comfortable, except for when an eighteen-wheeler drove by and the sidewalk shook.

The time I spent on Skid Row also showed me the underside of Los Angeles, so that whenever I see homeless people camped in tents along side streets or under overpasses, I have some understanding of what they are going through. In 1989, I wrote an article for the school paper (of Loyola Marymount University) about our obligation to help them that included this sentence: "Some of us are chasing fashions, acquiring rich men's toys, and riding our fancy limos over concrete pillars of fast freeways and high-rise ambitions, under which our hungry brother sits shivering."

Eventually, my desire to make the world a better place—or at least to improve the small part of it that I could make better—led me to become a teacher. I came to believe, as I still do, that it was the noblest and most important work in the world—not necessarily the most respected or the best paid but the noblest and most important. After my stint with the Catholic Worker community in Boyle Heights and at their soup kitchen in the heart of Skid Row, I started pursuing teaching positions. In January 1990, I became a substitute teacher for LAUSD and began working toward my credential, finally completing it in the fall of 1991. I had vainly hoped that one and a half years of subbing would lead to a full-time position, but when it didn't, I applied for positions at private schools. I was hired at a Catholic high school in the Fairfax area, several blocks south of Hollywood Boulevard and the Walk of Fame. This school, which has since closed, was located at the corner of Third and Detroit, one block west of La Brea. During my first year there, I commuted from Torrance. After that, I decided to eliminate my long drive by renting a studio apartment about a block north of the famed Chinese Theatre on Hollywood Boulevard. I lived there for a year, until I decided to teach for a year in Santiago de Compostela, Spain. I had a Honda CB700 Nighthawk motorcycle that I used to get around, and when I had holiday breaks from my teaching job, I traveled all over Western Europe on the motorcycle.

After returning to my parents' home in Torrance, I finally achieved a teaching position with LAUSD, but it was in the San Fernando Valley. I moved to the eastern part of the valley and started working in Sun Valley, just north of North Hollywood and right next to Sunland, Pacoima, and Arleta. After two years, I met the woman who would become my true love and my wife. We married in 1996 and bought a little house in North Hollywood less than a mile from the high school where I was teaching, Francis Polytechnic, on Roscoe Boulevard. Four years later, after my pay was augmented by raises granted because of a master's degree from Cal State Northridge and National Board Certification and after we started to be blessed with children, we looked for a bigger house to fill with our growing family. In 2001, we found one in Castaic, where we have lived since that time.

All the negative things I saw about LA during my adolescence are still around, but as I grew older, I learned about the more positive and interesting aspects of LA: the fascinating local history, the arts and entertainment, and the people—the workers, bartenders, students, actors, writers, directors, educators, counselors, nurses, pilots, service workers, and retirees I have gotten to know. Not everyone is happy or even friendly, but every person—or at least, *almost* every person—is interesting to chat with and get to know a bit. I stayed here because this is where my family and friends were and are. It's my home: my sweet and sour home. It's where I became a teacher, a local history nerd, a college instructor, and a rideshare driver. I am Lyfting LA.

5

DRUGS AND ALCOHOL ON THE STREETS OF LA

I'm an occasional drinker, the kind of guy who goes out for a beer and wakes up in Singapore with a full beard.

—Raymond Chandler

WHEN I WAS a high school and college student, I had friends who (like everyone else) often partied with alcohol, marijuana, and sometimes harder substances like cocaine, acid, or speed. I never participated much myself, except for alcohol occasionally and marijuana one time. I was sort of the token nerd who hung out with the cool people. They were my friends, so I spent a lot of time with them and didn't try to make them stop what they were doing, but they also accepted that I wasn't into it, so when the hash pipe or the bong was being passed around, they usually skipped me. I suppose you could say I grew up around the drug culture, but I was never really part of it. Perhaps this prepared me for my adult work as a high school teacher and a Lyft driver.

As any Lyft or Uber driver knows, many of the people who need a ride home late at night are drunk or stoned. Sometimes when passengers get in the car, there's an immediate smell of marijuana or hard liquor. Other times there's no smell, but the person is clearly high on shrooms or some other hallucinogenic substance. How does a driver know? A lot of times, the customers say so (between giggles and/or partially incoherent speech): "Dude, I just had some shrooms, and I'm feeling so crazy right now!" Other times, passengers will talk about what they used to do when they were younger. One middle-aged man told me that he used to get his illegal drugs from dealers who worked as valet drivers. I'm not sure how, but there was a secret understanding between customers and valet drivers at certain places. The customers would buy drugs from dealers who would park their cars and somehow give them drugs as they returned their car later.

A driver never knows for sure, but there were a few times when I gave rides that may have been part of a drug deal. One time, in the area of South Central LA (sometimes now called South LA), I had a passenger who asked me to pull over at several different locations, one at a time, and each stop lasted about two to three minutes. One stop was a 7-Eleven, then a private residence, then a small restaurant, then a hair salon, then another private residence. Each time, he would go inside, disappear for a few minutes, then come back out. I wasn't used to this kind of behavior from a passenger, so a couple of times, I almost tapped the button on the app that would have ended the ride, but then he came out again and assured me that his next stop would be really fast. Maybe he was just a popular guy with a lot of friends who liked to greet him for a few minutes—or maybe I was unwittingly assisting someone in a series of drug deals. As I said, a driver never knows for sure.

Another time, I picked up a young man at a palatial house at the top of a hill in a wealthy neighborhood with really nice homes and breathtaking views of the city. He carried a tote bag as he got in the car and didn't seem to want to enter into conversation, though he was friendly enough and answered harmless questions about the weather and how he was doing. We descended a series of winding roads, surrounded by homes that just screamed, "I am rich!" Eventually, we made it to ground level, and after a few more blocks, we turned a corner and ended up in an alley surrounded by apartment buildings and walls filled with graffiti. In other words, we had left the houses of the rich and famous (or at least the rich) and ended up in the heart of the hood. A small group of young men was standing in the otherwise deserted alley, apparently waiting for my passenger. He said, "Okay, thanks. I can get out here." I stopped the car, and he grabbed his tote bag, got out, and walked up to the group. They seemed glad to see him. Maybe they were just happy to see his tote bag. Again, a driver never knows for sure.

What's far more frequent than the apparent drug deals are the late-night rides for people who are drunk or tipsy. Sometimes a turn in the conversation can cause them to act a lot less tipsy. One time I picked up three young women from a bar between 11:00 p.m. and midnight, if memory serves. When they first got in the car, they were talking loudly and laughing with a devil-may-care attitude. As we drove through the darkness, they started conversing with me and found out that I was a teacher. One of them mentioned that she was also a teacher. As I soon learned, it just so happened that she taught at a school near my home and had had one of my children in her class. Her behavior suddenly changed, and she became a lot more businesslike once she realized that her Lyft driver was also the parent of one of the students at her school. I didn't mean to make her feel nervous or anything. It was amazing how quickly she recovered from the effects of alcohol. She told me how my son had done in her class. It was gratifying to learn that she thought he was really bright and that he could dominate his peers in a classroom debate. But it was awkward, and I felt a bit sorry for her that she had to put on her teacher hat when she was just blowing off steam with friends at a bar.

Another time I listened to a middle-aged man who had been unlucky in love. As he vented about his loneliness and his failure to find the right woman, he said that maybe he just needed to understand that he wasn't meant to be with anyone. After a divorce and several relationships that had ended badly, he said he should just learn to be happy with his dog and his friends. I remember the bitterness as he said, "Instead of going through another divorce, maybe I should just find a woman who hates me, give her my car and my house, and be done with it." I sure felt sorry for the guy. As I dropped him off, I asked if he was going to be all right. He responded by waving his hand behind him, and I watched him stumble up to his door. I said a prayer that things would improve for him soon.

It's not always that sad. Sometimes there are groups of friends who are going to or from places where they have (or had) a great time together, and I hear them discussing the fun they had and the places they've been. I remember hearing about a place that has different sections of themed rooms based on bygone decades: a 1920s section, a 1960s section, and a 1980s area. There are beer gardens or wine tasting events near the Los Angeles Zoo, in Little Tokyo, in Koreatown, in Marina Del Rey, and in many other places. Rideshare drivers provide a tremendously valuable service by getting people home safely after they visit these places or attend these events.

I've learned about the world of alcoholic drinks when I listen to passengers who are bartenders. One St. Patrick's Day, I was told that Irish coffee is not something people ask for much these days, even in Irish pubs. This was a bit of a disappointment for me, since I enjoyed Irish coffee when I visited Ireland in the nineties. I also learned that each whiskey (Jim Beam, Jack Daniel's, Kentucky bourbon, etc.) is made in a certain place that brews it in a particular way, and that's what gives it its own unique flavor. And the tequila with the worm in it is only brewed in one place in Mexico: a town named Tequila, in the state of Jalisco. Real champagne is made only in the city of Champagne, France.

I've also learned that there is an art to mixing drinks and that each bartender brings their own unique style to what they do. They sometimes develop a following, just as a rock star or a celebrity does, even if it's not on the same scale. I'm always glad when my passenger turns out to be a bartender. They're some of the most friendly and interesting people, and they almost always give a generous cash tip, probably because they know what it means to get a good tip while you're on the job.

One of the strangest conversations happened when I picked up three cheerful young men after a hockey game near downtown LA. Apparently, they ran a very lucrative cannabis business, and they were talking and laughing about a recent visit by members of the law enforcement community. I wasn't clear if they were referring to local law enforcement, the FBI, or the ATF. But every so often, a raid of their pot shop takes place. They know about it ahead of time, so they prepare before it happens.

At some point, they laughed and asked me if I knew what they were talking about. I said, "I think so. But I thought selling cannabis was legal now." I thought for moment. "But I guess some dispensaries are legal and some aren't." After a moment of silence, they started laughing again.

"I think he's getting it now!" There was more laughter.

"So the cops raid your pot shop," I asked, "but you know about it ahead of time?"

"That's right."

"How do you know about it?"

"We have a friend on the inside who tips us off," one of them said. I supposed he was referring to a paid informant who works in law enforcement.

"Okay," I continued, "so you know they're coming. How do you prepare? Do you hide all the cannabis?"

"No. That would be too obvious. We hide most of it, but we leave enough for them to seize and feel like they shut us down. Then we wait for a bit, restock, and reopen."

"Why don't you just change locations?"

"Because our clients know where we are, and we're making too much money to want to change things. So we let the dudes with the badges come in and do their raid once in a while, and then we go right back to business the next day. We're making so much, it's ridiculous!" They laughed again. It was clear to me that these were three young men who were making a lot of money and enjoying it. They talked about all the sports games they were able to attend, the places they traveled, and the women they dated.

But beneath all the laughter and positivity, there seemed a kind of uneasiness. It was like something was missing, or perhaps they felt some kind of guilt about all the easy money they were making. After all, many, if not most, of the people who patronized their business were probably engaging in some form of self-destructive behavior. Even if they were getting rich, maybe they had some doubts about what they were doing.

We came to the end of the ride. I still remember the last thing one of them said to me before getting out of the car. "I'm just trying to make a living, Larry, the same as anyone else. I'm just paying my bills and living my life." I wished him and his buddies well and drove off into the night.

There are a lot of drugs and alcohol on the streets of LA, but I'm not involved in it. I'm just one of the guys who gets you home safely after you've had a drink, smoked some weed, or done some lines. It's not my job to reform the souls of my passengers. But sometimes I do pray for them.

Several months after the educational ride with the three rich young entrepreneurs, I heard from the other side. This woman was going home from her job as a manager at a fully legal CBD store. I asked her about what she did, and she said she sells CBD products but only the kind that are fully legal and, in her words, fully safe. I mentioned my previous conversation with the three young men who were part of the illegal cannabis market, and she got somewhat indignant, not really against me but against the guys who were not present when we were speaking.

"Yeah, the stuff they sell is cheaper, but it's a lot more dangerous, too. You don't know where it's made, who's making it, or what they put into it."

"That's true," I said. "I've read about accidental overdoses where somebody tried an illegal drug, and it was laced with fentanyl or something similar that can cause death."

"Yeah, nobody's controlling it," she added, "so it might have something that can kill you or turn you into an addict."

"So even though they legalized weed," I said, "there's still a big illegal market?"

"That's right," she responded, "and it's really sad because a lot of people go to them because it's cheaper, but if you want to do the safe and responsible thing, you go to a shop like ours."

About that time, we reached her home.

"Okay," I said, "I'll keep that in mind. Nice talking with you."

"You, too," she replied. "Maybe we'll see you at our shop over on Ventura Boulevard. Have a nice day!"

6

THE HOMELESS ROMEO AND OTHER COUNSELING SESSIONS

When we turn to one another for counsel we reduce the number of our enemies.

—Khalil Gibran

ONE ASPECT OF rideshare driving that makes it a wonderful occupation for observers of humanity is that people from all levels of society use it (with the possible exception of the extremely rich). But even the employees and servicers of the extremely rich sometimes use it. So do their neighbors, in-laws, handlers, and associates in country clubs, cafés, bistros, and nightclubs. I have never met Arnold Schwarzenegger, Angelica Huston, Scarlett Johansson, or Ellen DeGeneres, but I've been the Lyft driver for people who have hung out with them, done their laundry, or worked as their personal assistant.

I've also given rides to teenagers and undocumented workers of all ages who are employed at fast-food places, such as McDonald's or Kentucky Fried Chicken, or as nannies in Brentwood or Beverly Hills. After their workday, they return to their homes in Inglewood, Compton, or East LA. And sometimes my passengers have been homeless people.

One young Black man got into my car in downtown LA and took a ride that lasted about fifteen minutes to Pasadena. We got to talking, and he told me about his situation. I played life counselor in a way that I hope caused a profound change in his life for the better.

He told me about the girl he was dating, who was the love of his life, and how much he was afraid of losing her. He said that before he met her, he had spent years without seriously dating anyone, and he never thought someone so beautiful and sweet as she could ever love *him*. But now this lovely goddess was spending time with him and telling him how much she loved him. He was almost unsure what to do with his amazing good fortune. And he was nervous as hell that he would make the wrong move and end up losing her.

"Why?" I asked him. "What are you afraid of?"

"If she gets to know too much about me, she might dump me."

"What do you mean? I thought that if you really love someone, the more you know about them, the more you love them. Isn't that what it means to really love someone—that you know their faults and you still love them?"

"Well, yeah, of course, man. But what if there's something you've never told them that you should have told them? And the longer you haven't, the more you feel trapped that you should have, but you haven't."

"What, are you a hit man for the mafia or something?"

"No," he said, laughing softly. "I work for the same company she does."

"Oh, you do? That's cool. How long have you worked there?"

"About five years."

"That's great! So you have a steady job and they like you."

"Yeah, but I don't have my own place."

"Do you have roommates or something?"

"No, man. I've been living on the sidewalk. I'm homeless, bro."

"So you have a steady job, but you don't have a steady home?"

"That's it, man. And that's what I'm afraid of telling her. She sees me at work. She knows I'm a responsible guy and a good worker. But she doesn't know I'm homeless. And I don't know how to tell her."

"Okay, so you're thinking that if she finds out your situation, she's not going to want to be with you anymore."

"That's it, man."

I thought for a moment, then an idea came to me. "I know what I would do if I were you," I said. "The next time you're with her, tell her about a friend of yours who's dating a woman he really loves—the woman of his dreams. But your friend has a problem. Even though he has a good job, he can't afford his own home yet, and he's afraid to tell the woman he loves about his situation. See what her reaction is. If she says, 'Eww, that's so gross,' then you have an idea of what she'll think. If she says that it shouldn't matter if he can't afford his own place, as long as they really love each other, then you could probably break it to her that your friend is actually you."

"Hey," he said, "I really like that idea. That's what I'm going to do."

Soon after that, we reached his destination. As he got out, he said, "Thanks again for the great advice, and God bless you, sir."

I bid him farewell and wished him the best of luck. If it so happens that the homeless Romeo ever reads this, I'd love it if you could email me (*lyftinglawriter@gmail.com*) to let me know how things turned out.

*   *   *

Another time, I responded to a ride request from a Starbucks in Santa Monica. As I approached, I noticed two lovely young women wearing classy-looking dresses standing on the sidewalk. As I pulled up to the curb, they opened the door. Sure enough, it was one of them who had requested the ride. As we proceeded to their destination, I gathered that they were old friends, and one of them had been working in a city back east (perhaps it was Philadelphia). She was visiting the other, whom, I presumed, still lived and worked in Southern California. They were discussing men and relationships, and when two longtime female friends talk about these topics, I usually stay out of the conversation unless invited to chime in. I don't remember how, but at some point they asked for my opinion.

As I remember, the situation was that one of them had been dating a young man for a few months, and he had recently told her that he loved her. She was trying to decide how to interpret and respond to what he had said. The problem, I pointed out, is that the word *love* means so many different things to different people. Unfortunately, when a young man says that in today's society, it could mean "I'm attracted to you, and I want to sleep with you" without any kind of commitment or willingness to stay around after the party's over. On the other hand, it could be a sincere statement of a desire to make the young woman his one and only and to be committed in a lasting relationship, which would find its fulfillment in marriage.

"So my advice," I said, "would be to ask him what he means when he says he loves you. Because different guys mean different things when they say that."

"Are you married?" one of them asked.

"Yes, I am and have been for almost twenty-five years now."

"That's great!" they both exclaimed. Then one said, "That's really nice that you guys have stayed together so long."

"Do you have children?" asked the other one.

"Yes, we have five, and they weren't accidents!" They both laughed. Then I explained, "Before we got married, we agreed that we'd like to have a bigger family than the average two children."

"That's really nice," they said.

"But getting back to what we were talking about," I continued, "I didn't find the right person until I was thirty-one. And I learned long before that that just saying 'I love you' doesn't settle everything. In fact, it usually creates more questions than it answers. Two people might love each other very much, but if they can't agree on how they would want to spend their lives together, including the questions of children and how many they would be willing to raise together, sometimes it's best if they don't let 'I love you' turn into a serious commitment."

"Wow," said one of the young women, "it seems like you know a lot. Do you have another job you do besides Lyft?"

"I teach at a high school and a community college."

"I knew it! What do you teach?"

"English."

"That's really nice. My aunt's a teacher."

"Is she? Around here?"

"No, she teaches in Boston. But she really enjoys her job. I bet you do, too."

"Sometimes I do. But sometimes I like to be away from it, too. Driving for Lyft has opened up a whole new world—actually, several whole new worlds!"

We reached their destination at about that time, so I pulled up and stopped. We said our farewells, and they got out. I remember hoping, almost like a father parting from his daughters, that they would be loved and cherished and respected by the men in their lives.

7

THE LIFE COACH, AD HOC THERAPIST, CHEERLEADER, AND BARTENDER IS IN

ONE OF THE coolest things about working as a rideshare driver is what might be called the bartender aspect. Various passengers tend to say anything and everything about their lives to a bartender, because they're a fairly safe person in whom to confide. Generally, a bartender is someone who is not directly involved in one's personal life, and in feuds at home or at work, but is willing to listen and sympathize with whatever is going on in another's life. And so people tend to talk with and open up to their bartenders. Perhaps the fact that they are drinking alcohol also contributes to their freedom of self-expression.

Although I have never served alcohol to my passengers, I have often listened to their stories and sometimes offered advice that seemed valuable to them. I once picked up an airline pilot at an airport and gave him a ride to his home in a nice suburban neighborhood not far from Mulholland Drive. As we talked, we discovered that we were both fathers of teenagers. My older children were already young adults, but my two youngest children were still in their teen years. By contrast, my pilot passenger had two daughters, one who had recently become a teenager and a younger one who was a preteen. He described the older daughter as wonderful and doing very well in school and getting along very well with her family. However, the younger one was impossible and sometimes unwilling to listen to her mother. "How do you deal with that?" he asked.

I asked him if the troublesome daughter got along with him. He said, "Sure, we get along great, but sometimes I'm gone for several days at a time, because I'm flying all over the planet."

"One thing I've found," I said, "in dealing with the daughters I've been raising is that sometimes they'll listen to me, even if they don't seem to listen to their mom. It might be because I'm also out working a lot, both as a teacher and as a rideshare driver. But when I take the time to speak with one of my daughters (or sons) one-on-one, we usually have a pretty good talk. I guess what I'm saying is that if your daughter is having an issue with your wife, the solution might be for you to spend some time with her, maybe take her out for some frozen yogurt or something, and talk with her about whatever the problem is."

He seemed thoughtful for a moment. "Maybe you're right. I suppose I could try to talk with her once in a while when she's being impossible with her mother."

"I'm not sure why it is, but it seems like both boys and girls reach a certain age in which they don't seem as willing to listen to their mother, but they'll still listen to their father. Of course, they should always listen to both, but if they don't, then the solution is sometimes making some one-on-one father and child time."

"That's a pretty good idea," he said. "I think I'll try that with Isabel." Not long after that, we arrived at his home. He thanked me and got out, walking to the front door of a nice, well-kept house.

*   *   *

Then there was the time I picked up a fellow educator who was about to make her debut on a cable TV show. She was a preschool teacher who told me that she was nervous, because after she spent some time with some friends for the evening, she would return home, go to sleep, and get up early to go to the studio of the cable channel she would be on (it may have been Nickelodeon, but I'm not sure).

"So tomorrow morning," I asked her, "you're going to be on a cable TV show?"

"Yes," she said, "with kids."

"With kids?"

"Yes. I actually have to teach a lesson, just like I would in my classroom."

"So you're going to be teaching a lesson, with actual kids, on TV?"

"That's right."

"Okay, I can see why you're nervous."

She laughed. "Do you have any advice for me?"

I thought for a moment. "It's been a long time since I've done any acting, but I did play the lead part in the fall production of my high school."

"You did? That's really cool! What play was it?"

"Agatha Christie's *The Mousetrap*."

"You didn't have problems with stage fright?"

"Not really. I mean, I was nervous about being on a stage in front of a few hundred people, but I remember something I did that worked for me."

"What was that?"

"I completely shut the audience out of my mind. I just focused on the character or characters to whom I was speaking or on what my character was thinking or feeling. I pretended that the audience wasn't there. I tried not to think about them."

"And that worked?"

"It did for me," I told her. "When you're teaching students, the best thing you could do, I think, is to focus on the kids you're helping and to be as attentive and caring toward each one as you would be if you were in your classroom. Don't think about the camera or the people watching. Don't give any thought to anyone else except the kids you're teaching, and don't think about anything else except what you're helping them to learn. If you don't think of yourself as nervous, you'll seem like you're not nervous. Does that make sense?"

"Yes, it does, absolutely! I'm going to do that tomorrow morning. Thank you so much." At about this point, we reached her destination.

"What's the name of the show?" I asked her. She told me, but unfortunately, I can't recall it. "I'm sure you'll do fine."

"Thanks again! I really appreciate it."

The next morning she did the show, and it was a smashing success . . . right?

*　　*　　*

Another time, I picked up a young man near Pier Avenue in Hermosa Beach. This area has a lot of bars and clubs that feature live bands, and so in the evening, especially on weekends, it's usually crowded and full of young people walking around, going in or coming out of bars, clubs, and restaurants. I observed a young man approaching the car, then he stopped. He looked back and around anxiously, then shrugged and got in.

I greeted him as I usually do to make sure he was the intended passenger. He responded cordially but was clearly not in a good mood. As we drove toward his destination, he exclaimed, "I can't believe he ditched me! He's such an asshole!"

"I'm sorry," I replied, not knowing what to say.

"It's like he was just telling me what a special person I am to him, and then he just leaves me at the club and doesn't respond to my calls and texts."

We drove on through the night. "So do you have a significant other?"

"Yes, I've been married for about twenty-five years."

"Twenty-five years! Wow, you must really love your wife."

"Yeah, I do. We have our ups and downs, but we love each other and our kids."

"Oh! You have kids. How many?"

"I have five."

"Five kids? That's a big family!"

"Yeah. I guess it keeps me out of trouble. That's also why I drive for Lyft."

"How did you know your wife was the one for you?"

"Well, I remember when I met her, I thought she was really cute. Then I asked some friends about her, and they gave me some advice, then I gave her a call, and eventually we started dating, and things just worked out. I came to believe that it was God's will for us to be together and that she was meant for me."

"That's really sweet," he said. "I don't know if I'll ever find one person who's right for me."

"It didn't happen for me until I was thirty-one. It'll happen for you when it's meant to be. Until then, it's probably best not to try too hard. Sometimes if you try too hard for something, you end up pushing it away."

"Oh, that's for sure!" he said. "I thought this guy was going to be mine, and then he just ditches me. He's such a jerk."

"So I guess you're better off without him, huh?"

"You said it." His phone started to ring. "Oh, that's my mom. Sorry, I better answer this." He put his cell phone to his ear. "*¡Hola, Corazón!*" Then I heard the sound of a woman speaking Spanish on the other end of the call. "*Si, Mami. Lo siento.*" I listened as he explained to his mom that he was sorry he had not been at a party she wanted him to attend. He asked her not to worry about him and assured her lovingly that he would be fine and that he would try to be there next time she wanted him to be somewhere. As I listened to him speaking so tenderly and affectionately to his mother, I got to really like him. When a grown man shows that much love for his mother, there has to be at least *some* good in him.

He finished the call, then resumed talking with me. I got the uncomfortable feeling that he was trying to hit on me, so I tried to make it clear that I was quite happy with my wife and not into dudes.

We pulled up at his destination and his phone rang again. "I can't believe it!"

"What?"

"It's him."

"Who?"

"Reggie! The guy who ditched me." He answered the phone. "Yeah, what do you want?" I heard a man's voice on the other end. "I left about twenty minutes ago!" I heard the voice again. "Because you ditched me, and you didn't respond to my calls and texts!" Then, after the voice spoke again, "That's okay. I'm at home now, and my Lyft driver is a really nice guy." I turned back to look at him, and he made a motion with his hand as if to say, "Just play along with it."

For a moment I hesitated, unsure of whether I should participate in his game. I had been taught that homosexual behavior was sinful, and so I wasn't sure if it would be right to act as an enabler. But then I thought about how he was really nice to his mother and how he was still my passenger and that maybe I should try to accommodate his wishes.

So when he said into the phone, "We're doing just fine, aren't we, Larry?" I responded with a loud, deep-voiced, "Yeah!" Not long after that, he got out of the car and thanked me for my assistance. I'm not sure, but I think he remained on the phone as he walked up to his home. Perhaps he worked it out with his friend, perhaps not. I probably said a prayer for his soul and drove off to the next ride.

*   *   *

Once I got a request from a rich neighborhood of hilltop homes overlooking the 405 Freeway, nestled between the Getty Center and the Skirball Center. I pulled up at a very expensive-looking home, and an Asian man got in. We started talking, and he said that he was going to watch a soccer game between Mexico and South Korea. But this wasn't a live game; it was a telecast on a very big screen at a place near downtown LA.

There are several buildings near downtown that look as if they were abandoned warehouses that are now experiencing their second wind as clubs, bars, or little side street cafés. Some urban planners call this gentrification. It was to one of these that I was headed with my Korean soccer fan. As we pulled into the parking lot next to the former warehouse-looking building, we saw a large number of people getting out of cars and walking inside. Almost all of them were wearing green and gold colors, but a few—perhaps about one in twenty or thirty—were wearing reddish-orange and white, the colors of the Korean team. My passenger said, "All of these people are going to watch the game, just like me. But most of them are cheering for the Mexican team." He joked, "I hope I don't get beaten up!"

We pulled up to the area where rideshare passengers were supposed to be dropped off. I asked, "Are you going to be okay?"

"I'll be fine," he said.

"You know, I'm part Asian," I said, "so I guess I should cheer for the Korean team."

He smiled and thanked me as he got out of the car. "We'll see what happens. Have a good day!"

Almost immediately, I got a request from someone a few miles away. I tapped the symbol to accept the request and drove to where the passenger was waiting. It was an older Mexican gentleman who didn't speak a word of English (or if he did, he didn't admit it), so I conversed with him in Spanish. I soon learned that he was heading for the same soccer game viewing event where I had just dropped off the Korean gentleman. It was a much shorter ride, so we didn't have a lot of time to talk, but when it was time to drop him off, I decided to give him a friendly, encouraging word: "¡*Viva Mexico!*"

His face brightened, and he responded enthusiastically, "¡*Oh si! Viva Mexico! Gracias, señor.*"

As he walked toward the building, I remember feeling glad that I was able to bring joy to a passenger's life. But I also felt a bit awkward, since I had just indicated support for the opposite team about twenty minutes beforehand, in the same parking lot. I questioned myself: Was I a sellout? Was I prostituting my loyalties for the approval of the latest passenger? Nah. I don't think so. A good Lyft driver always makes his passengers feel comfortable and supported. If you're my passenger, and you're a sports fan, I'll cheer for your team—even if it means cheering for both sides on the same morning!

8

LYFTING THE STARS AND THOSE WHO WORK WITH THEM

ONE OF THE coolest things that sometimes happens while ride-share driving in the Los Angeles area is the occasional ride that you give to an interesting celebrity or to someone who works with them. I remember picking up a woman near the Warner Brothers Studios in Burbank who spoke about her work as a personal assistant to Ellen DeGeneres. She mentioned that Ellen is a genuinely nice person to work for.

Several times I have given rides to people whose names I was not familiar with, but after they told me about their work, I googled them later and learned more about them. Once I picked up a sort of nerdy-looking young man in front of the Comedy Store on Sunset Boulevard and asked if he had enjoyed the show. "Did you laugh a lot? Was it funny?"

He replied, "It was all right, I guess."

I asked, "But did it make you laugh?"

"Not really."

"No? Why not?"

"Well, because I was the comedian. I think I made the audience laugh, though."

"Oh, okay. So you were the comedian. I wonder if I've heard of you. What's your name?"

"I'm Tommy Ryman."

We continued our conversation in the course of the ride between Sunset Strip and his destination in the South Bay. I was impressed by how friendly and likeable he was, even though he had achieved some degree of fame and success in the world of comedy. When I told him that I'd be sure to check out his routines on YouTube but that I wasn't sure if I would let my kids watch them (assuming that a successful comedian was probably raunchy or racy in his act), I was pleasantly surprised to hear him respond that he keeps his routines clean. I was even more impressed when I got home and watched some clips. Later, I showed them to my children, and we had some good laughs.

Four times (that I can recall; there may have been more) I had a pleasant conversation with cover girl models whose stature I realized only after verifying that they were as big as they said they were. Because I'm a happily married man (and have been for more than twenty years now), I've never tried to start any kind of relationship with anyone else. That's one reason why I'm not mentioning any names in this paragraph.

Another time, I picked up a very likeable young man who had been a regular on the TV show *Days of Our Lives* for about six years. I found out more information about Brendan Coughlin on IMDB (Internet Movie Database). In the course of our friendly conversation, he mentioned his work in TV and movies. As we talked about the acting and entertainment industry, which is sometimes referred to by Angelenos as simply the industry, I mentioned that a couple of people in my family are successful on-screen personalities but that they're still kind and considerate toward others.

Brendan opined how it's great when people can make it big in the movies and still be nice, down-to-earth, relatable people. After a few more minutes, we reached Brendan's destination, so we said our farewells and he got out.

A few months after the conversation with Brendan, I was driving a gentleman who worked as a casting director. I don't recall his name, but when he mentioned some of the films he had worked on, they were big movies that I had either seen or heard of.

A few months after that, I picked up a charming thirtysomething couple somewhere in Pasadena. During the ride, they started speaking about a TV show that had just been canceled after two seasons. It was called *Kevin Can Wait*, and I recall the husband saying to his wife, "I'm sure it breaks your heart." I detected just a bit of sarcasm in his statement.

His wife replied, "Yeah, I'm crushed. After they were so nice to me."

He said, "Well, they got what they deserved."

I became curious about the meaning of some of their seemingly strange statements, so I asked them about it. They explained that she had been a regular on the show, but she had been fired, along with several others, for no good reason. She said, "It seems like karma that the show got canceled. But I do feel sorry for all the people who had good work and who are now unemployed or having to look elsewhere for work."

"Well, there are a lot of projects going on in the industry out there. One thing about my years of driving for Lyft: I drive all kinds of people who work on all kinds of shows as camera operators, makeup artists, screenwriters, actors, you name it."

"That's true," she said. "But there was no good reason they had to fire us like that. The show was doing well, we were working together well, then they had to go and ruin it."

I said, "I'm sorry that happened, but hopefully you get to do some other great work on other shows." Her husband concurred, and soon we reached their destination. Before we stopped, I asked if she wouldn't mind telling me her name, and she did.

Later, when I got home, I researched the cancellation of *Kevin Can Wait* as well as the name of the actress with whom I had spoken. I learned information about both, including this headline, which appeared on Yahoo! Entertainment (originally on TVLine. com): "*Kevin Can Wait* Cancelled at CBS After Polarizing Season 2 Shake-Up."[1] I also recognized the actor who played the title character, Kevin James, from the *Mall Cop* films in which he also played the title character, Paul Blart. Those movies are two of my favorite comedies, and they don't have anything offensive or inappropriate, so I can watch them with my young children.

I would say the same about the *Guardians of the Galaxy* films. The humor is very funny and the characterization is endearing, but there's nothing that would be inappropriate to watch with children. I remember another conversation I had with a tech guy who worked on special effects in films. He mentioned that somebody at Disney had made the decision to fire the brain behind the *Guardians of the Galaxy* films, James Gunn, over some offensive tweets he had made several years back. He said, "You'd think that once a guy said he was sorry, they'd let it go."

---

1   Ryan Schwartz, "*Kevin Can Wait* Cancelled at CBS After Polarizing Season 2 Shake-Up," TVLine.com, May 12, 2018, https://tvline.com/news/kevin-can-wait-cancelled-season-3-cbs-945036.

"I know," I responded. "And it was because of tweets that were years old and attempts at humor. It's not like he just tweeted them and was doubling down on what he said."

"They'll never get the kind of work they got from Gunn," he opined. "Whoever they bring in to replace him . . . it won't be the same."

I agreed and dropped off the tech guy. We both felt of sense of sadness that there wouldn't be another *Guardians* film directed by James Gunn. Sometime afterward, I had a similar conversation with another tech guy. This time, there was a happy ending to our discussion: He said that Gunn had been hired back. The studio had reversed its decision, and he was rehired to work on the third film in the series. I was very happy to hear this. I googled the subject and found this statement from James Gunn: "I am tremendously grateful to every person who has supported me over the past few months. I am always learning and will continue to work at being the best human being I can be. I deeply appreciate Disney's decision and I am excited to continue making films that investigate the ties of love that bind us all. I have been, and continue to be, incredibly humbled by your love and support. From the bottom of my heart, thank you. Love to you all."[2]

There are enough stories of heartbreak and broken dreams in Hollywood that it's nice when a story has a happy ending.

---

2   Brian Welk, "James Gunn Thanks Disney for His 'Guardians' Return: 'I Am Always Learning,'" TheWrap, March 15, 2019, www.thewrap.com/james-gunn-thanks-disney-for-his-guardians-return-i-am-always-learning.

9

THE COOLEST RIDE EVER

Spread love everywhere you go: Let no one ever come to you without leaving happier.

—Mother Teresa of Calcutta

EVERY LYFT OR Uber driver has a story about their coolest ride. Mine began on an August evening near the Hollywood Bowl, just after a concert. I received a request just as the area was going crazy with thousands of people leaving. I maneuvered through heavy traffic to park as close as I could near the big sign just off Highland Boulevard. Then I called the passenger to see if he was nearby.

When the gentleman answered, he told me where he was. I told him where I was and that I didn't think I could get much closer. He replied, "Okay, I think I know where you are. We'll come down the hill."

I waited for a few minutes. He called back and said, "We don't see you. Where are you again?"

I told him I was just beyond the big sign in the Odin parking lot. I was beginning to have my doubts that they would find me, but just then a man and a woman recognized me and approached my car. The gentleman opened the door for the woman, and she got in. I greeted them both.

Soon we started driving to their destination. I asked them about the concert they attended, and they replied that they enjoyed it very much. I told them about the concert I had gone to at the Hollywood Bowl a few weeks previously: a screening of the 2009 *Star Trek* movie (directed by J. J. Abrams, which was my favorite of all the *Star Trek* films) with a live performance of the music from the film. The Los Angeles Philharmonic performed the music, accompanied by the Los Angeles Master Chorale, which performed the vocal parts, all while the film was shown on the screen. I mentioned how my children and I enjoyed the experience and how I had watched the original *Star Trek* TV series as a child in the 1970s.

This was what Mariette Hartley looked like when I first saw her as a child watching Star Trek.

In the only episode where Spock falls in love, Hartley played the girl he fell for.

As we spoke, the gentleman said to the woman, "You were in one of those episodes, weren't you?"

She said, "Yes. It was the only episode [of Season 3] where Spock falls in love with an alien."

"Really?" I said. "Yeah, it's usually Captain Kirk who fell for the female aliens. And of course it never worked out so that he could be free for the next episode!"

They chuckled politely. Then I asked the woman, "What was the name of the episode you were in?" I thought maybe she had a bit part, in which she stood in the background or walked by while the big stars were enacting a scene.

She replied, "The episode was called 'All Our Yesterdays.' I was Zarabeth." At the time, I didn't recall who Zarabeth was, so I wasn't yet aware of the person with whom I was speaking. "All Our Yesterdays" featured a planet that was about to be destroyed by its sun, so its inhabitants figure out a method of time travel to go back thousands of years into the past in order to survive. Spock goes back in time and experiences feelings the way Vulcans did before they learned to conquer their emotions with logic. And so he falls in love with a cave-girl named Zarabeth.

As the ride continued, I still hadn't recognized the person with whom I was speaking. I still thought I was talking with an extra who had a walk-on part for a few seconds in one episode of *Star Trek*.

In the course of our conversation, I mentioned to her and her husband that I was an English teacher, and they seemed really interested in what I told them about myself. After she mentioned the title "All Our Yesterdays," I told her that it was from Shakespeare's *Macbeth*. It was a line from the title character's soliloquy in Act 5, just after his wife's death is reported to him by a messenger:

> She should have died hereafter
> There would have been time for such a word.

Tomorrow and tomorrow and tomorrow,
Creeps in this petty pace from day to day
To the last syllable of recorded time,
And all our yesterdays have lighted fools
The way to dusty death. Out, out, brief candle!
Life's but a walking shadow, a poor player
That struts and frets his hour upon the stage
And then is heard no more: it is a tale
Told by an idiot, full of sound and fury,
Signifying nothing.

As we were speaking, I remember how Ms. Hartley and her husband were polite enough to act as if I was enlightening them, when in reality they probably knew Shakespeare backward and forward when I was still in grade school! I remember explaining how, when I taught *Macbeth*, I told the students that Macbeth's life had become meaningless because of the bad choices he made—to betray and murder his friends for power. Shakespeare wasn't saying that all life was meaningless; he was showing how life becomes meaningless for those who make bad choices. If Macbeth had lived a good life, he would have "that which should accompany old age: as honor, love, obedience, troops of friends," which, Macbeth says, "I may not look to have." They listened politely and seemed really interested in what I was saying.

We reached their destination. Ms. Hartley said, "Well, this was our first time trying Lyft, and we liked it!"

I told her I was glad and that it was a pleasure for me, as well. Then, as they were about to get out, I said, "May I ask your name?"

She said, "Sure. I'm Mariette Hartley."

I said, "You're Mariette Hartley? I used to watch you on TV when I was growing up!" I turned around and looked directly at her for the first time and recognized her face. "I'm sorry to be so clichéd, but may I have your autograph before you go?"

She said, "I'll do better than that. Just wait here for a minute." She went into her home, along with her husband. A few moments later, she emerged with a book, which she handed to me. "I think you might enjoy reading this." I looked at the book and saw that it was her autobiography.

"Thank you very much!" I said enthusiastically.

"You're welcome. Thanks again for the ride. Nice meeting you, Larry. Have a good evening."

When I got home, the first thing I did was watch "All Our Yesterdays" once more on a website that streams classic TV shows. Then I started reading Ms. Hartley's autobiography. I noticed that she had written "Dear Larry—Thanks for our sweet drive! Bless you and your beloved family! All the best, Mariette Hartley."

How could I *not* want to read a book in which the famous author had written such a kind and touching message just to me?

Over the next couple of weeks, I read her autobiography, *Breaking the Silence*. It was often funny, sometimes sad, sometimes profound, but always touching. The reader is invited into scenes from her awkward childhood, when she was treated cruelly at school and sometimes coldly by her mother. Hartley's mother was the daughter of Dr. John Watson, the influential psychologist and father of behaviorism, who spread the ridiculous idea that children should not be kissed or hugged as they are growing up. And yet, somehow, in spite of the influence of the wrongheaded theories of her influential grandfather, she had grown into the warm, caring person I met on an August evening in 2016.

She shares the triumphs and tragedies of her life as she started to make it in show business. As I read the rest of her autobiography, it struck me how each of the men in her early life had cast upon her some form of mental or physical abuse, and yet she refused to let the ill treatment she suffered define the essence of who she was. Her grandfather taught her mother (and, unfortunately, many other mothers of that era) that a child should not feel loved by his/her mother. And so she missed out on motherly affection as she was growing up. Later she would attempt to fill the void by allowing herself to be exploited, used, and abused by various men. She describes how her first husband beat her savagely several times. Then, after she got her father to escort her to acting jobs and after she filed for divorce, her abusive ex-husband continued to follow her around town and even sit in the audience of live TV tapings. I remember reading that part of the book and wishing I could jump into the story and rescue her from her abusive husband. A few years later, she was finally free of that creepy guy, thanks to a court order, but then her father succumbed to despair and ended his own life.

Her book is heart-wrenchingly sad at some points, and yet she maintains a sense of humor and a sort of wisdom through the suffering. Probably one of the funniest scenes is when she describes giving birth, surrounded by paramedics and cops, on a gurney, halfway in the birthing center and half on Washington Boulevard. It was heartwarming to follow her experiences as the wife of a Frenchman (who was *not* abusive but whose family and French ways would provide a significant amount of challenges and comedy for her) and as a mother of young children, balancing her acting career and the needs of her family. She writes,

> A lot of decisions are revocable. You take a job; you quit a job. You take a husband; you quit a husband. Deciding to have children is irrevocable. Once that tiny person pops out, you can't change your mind. There aren't any lemon laws to protect you. Say good-bye to entering a bathroom unaccompanied by a minor. Say good-bye to reading anything longer than milk of magnesia bottles. Say good-bye to sounding sane on friends' answering

machines. "Hi, luvey, it's moi, Mariette. I just wanted to call and say how much I missed you, and . . . stop it!"[3]

In the title of her book, she uses the phrase *breaking the silence*, which seemed uncannily prescient of the #MeToo movement that started in 2018, when the story finally broke of the abuses of movie mogul Harvey Weinstein. Hartley takes the reader through the ups and downs of her early life and shows us the person behind the successful actress she would become as she grew and developed in her field. Her story is a journey through heartbreaking sadness, disappointment, abandonment, and betrayal to a place of warmth, love, and success. Through her enjoyable autobiography, Hartley breaks the silence surrounding her early life and becomes an inspiring example of the words of Henry David Thoreau: "If one advances confidently in the direction of his dreams, and endeavors to live the life which he has imagined, he will meet with a success unexpected in common hours."

---

3   Mariette Hartley and Anne Commire, *Breaking the Silence* (New York: G. P. Putnam's Sons, 1990), X.

10

THE GODFATHER OF STUNT WORK IN SOCAL

WHO IS THE closest real-life example of Cliff Booth, the heroic
but fictional stunt double played by Brad Pitt in Quentin Tarantino's
Once upon a Time in Hollywood? Recently, I got to meet him. How
did this happen?

One evening, I picked him up—the man who turned out to be
the godfather of stunt work in the SoCal film and TV industry. He's
not the only one in that line of work, but he's the longest-serving

stuntman/stunt coordinator still alive and working in the industry, and he has achieved a legendary status among filmmakers in Hollywood and in the greater Los Angeles area. His name is Terry James, and everyone in the industry who deals with stuntmen (and stuntwomen) knows who he is. When I met him, he had been doing stunt work for forty years, had been a stunt double for some of the biggest stars, worked on some of the most iconic films and TV shows, and coordinated stunts for many others, including two of his sons, who followed him into the industry and who now do stunt work in their own careers. He also earned four Emmy Awards for his stunt work in TV shows.

Terry James, next to the four Emmy Awards he has earned for his stunt work.

This impressive, legendary guy was kind enough to agree to an interview at his home. I remember how once I got up the courage to text him and ask if he would be willing to be interviewed for my someday book, *Lyfting LA*, I was pleasantly surprised to see his answer. He texted back not just Okay but I'm all over it! I asked if he might be available on Thursday or Friday. He texted back that he was available on Thursday; Friday he was working. I would find out later that his work on Friday would be on the long-running show *The Young and the Restless*. This soap opera started in 1973 and had, by 2019, the ninth highest episode count of all TV programs in the world. But that was only the latest in a very impressive list of movies and television shows he had worked on in his long, multifaceted career.

Without further ado, here are some highlights of the interview. (LC is me; TJ is Terry James, a.k.a. the real Cliff Booth.)

* * *

LC: When did you first become a stuntman?

TJ: In 1979. I doubled Greg Evigan on *BJ and the Bear*. [There was a big fascination with trucking culture in the 1970s, with movies like *Smokey and the Bandit* and songs like "Convoy" and the Grateful Dead's "Truckin'" that were all the rage. *BJ and the Bear* was a popular TV series at the time that followed the adventures of a roving trucker and his pet monkey.]

LC: What made you interested in doing that?

TJ: I grew up with Roy Roger's son, Dusty Rogers [Roy Rogers Jr., whose parents were legendary country artists, Roy Rogers and Dale Evans]. Because I was always doing something crazy with bikes or jumping off a house or something, they kept telling me, "You should be a stuntman!"

LC: What city was that in?

TJ: That was here in Chatsworth. And then he graduated, and I went back to Ohio to live with my parents. He came with me, because his parents wanted him to get away from this girl he was with; they didn't like her. So [in Ohio] I introduced him to the woman he's married to today, and they've got kids. My aunt Erstine's dad was surgeon general under Roosevelt, and Jane Russell was her cousin. So using Jane Russell's name and Roy Roger's name got the doors open, but then I had to be able to perform. And when I was able to perform, it just went from there. I did *Knight Rider* with David Hasselhoff, and I did the movie *Stripes* and *Revenge of the Nerds*, and then my career just kicked off. [That's putting it mildly, as a quick look at the Terry James page on IMDB will show.]

LC: I know you doubled for Liam Neeson, David Hasselhoff, and Michael Madsen. Who are some other big names you've doubled for?

TJ: Jon Voight, Tab Hunter, John Schneider [one of the original *Dukes of Hazzard*]. I doubled Peter O'Toole.

LC: What did you do for Peter O'Toole?

TJ: It was a Paramount Picture [*The Seventh Coin*, 1993]. I was in Israel. They shipped me out in the middle of the night. I set my bags down [after landing] and looked around to see where I should go, and these guys showed up with Uzis and asked, "Where you goin'?" And they took my passport, papers, and everything. My hair had been bleached blond to double Peter O' Toole, and they put gray in it, and it didn't match my passport.

LC: They were Israeli soldiers?

TJ: Yes. After two and a half hours, they took my bags and walked me to the plane. I got on, and they closed the doors. It was crazy.

LC: What's the most dangerous job you've done?

TJ: The most dangerous was when I was doubling Liam Neeson on *Darkman* [1990] in downtown LA on six different days, every Saturday and Sunday for three weekends. It was like an unspoken understanding that when we did the test, if the helicopter ran into trouble, they had to cut me loose. They'd have to rotor down because I'd be ballast to them, and they would have to try to find a place to ditch it. I knew every time I got up there, there was a chance that something would happen, and they'd have to cut me loose.

LC: You didn't have a parachute or anything?

TJ: No, just a cable. The bottom line was I would take off, and the helicopter that was chasing us would take off, and then the camera helicopter. And so we took off and started going over the city, and then the other helicopter blew the motor and just came slamming down about forty feet, right to the ground. They brought me in and said, "That's it. Done for the day." They got all shook up. It could have been the helicopter *I* was on, you know? Those are the things in the back of your mind: It could be your last day. But I've been blessed.

LC: I saw that you worked on one of my all-time favorite films, *Glory* [1989, about one of the first Black regiments to serve in the Civil War, featuring Matthew Broderick and Cary Elwes and established Denzel Washington and Morgan Freeman as major stars]. As a teacher, I've used it in my classroom, when I was teaching American literature. What did you do in that film?

TJ: I did a bunch of huge fights, like where the Black soldiers were coming up the hill and there was shooting, and we were rolling down the hill. I got shot several times, but they made me up to look like different people.

LC: So you died a whole bunch of times! [Laughter]

TJ: [Laughter] Yeah . . . we did that on Jekyll Island, between Florida and Georgia.

LC: What was your worst injury?

TJ: I broke my back in 1983 doing a commercial. I went into an airbag standing up. I had to go past the camera standing up, because I was supposed to go off a train trestle and into the water. So they put the thing alongside the bridge, where the land was. I had to come down like I was going into the water. I couldn't dive or anything. I just had to jump feet first. And when I went into the airbag, I snapped my back.

LC: Jeez. Were you able to recover?

TJ: Yeah. But it took me a good six months. And I didn't know it was broken [at first].

LC: Have you ever had a dry spell or a tough time?

TJ: Oh yeah, probably 1988, I think it was. Everything came to a halt. I had to sell my house and buy another house so that I could recoup everything . . . and then I came out of it, but a lot of people didn't. A lot of people left the business at that point.

LC: Yeah, I guess for a lot of people in the industry, even after success, they're not sure where the next job will be.

TJ: Oh yeah, been there! [Laughter] I'm the longest-running stunt coordinator in the world. Nobody can beat my record. I've been on *The Young and the Restless* for thirty-one years! The closest guy was Mike Adams, who passed away about ten years ago, and he was about four or five years behind me.

LC: So would it be an exaggeration to call you the godfather of stunt work?

TJ: [Laughter] That's about right. I'm a legend. Everybody calls me a legend when they see me. I'm really not, but they call me that because of all the stuff I've done and where I've been.

LC: Got any good funny stories?

TJ: I did a thing called *Ultraman* [TV series, 1993–1994]. It was a Japanese thing, and I played about seven different characters in it. And so I had this big outfit on, with these wings and stuff, and I was walking through this city, this miniature town, crushing things, and then I was supposed to fly away. They have cables, and they have to take me up into the air. They said, "We're going to take you up at the end of the street." So I got there, and they took me up. Then they said, "That's a cut. We're going to lunch." They turned the lights off, and I was still at the top.

LC: They forgot about you?

TJ: [I yelled,] "Hey! Hey! What are you guys doing? Let me down!" About ten minutes later, they came back and asked, "Are you still up there?" Then they got me down.

LC: When I first talked with you [during the Lyft ride], you told me a funny story about David Hasselhoff.

TJ: We were doing *The SpongeBob SquarePants Movie* [2004], and I was dressed in a green outfit, and we got him [Hasselhoff] on a canoe, and he gets thrown over. They were just kind of like "Well, get over here and do this and do that," and I was like "Okay, no problem. You hired me to do this, and I'll do it." They put him in the canoe, and I'm at the end of the canoe, and he's looking at me, and he [Hasselhoff] goes, "Terry?" He shuts the whole crew down and says to his wife, "This is the guy I was telling you about! He doubled me on *Knight Rider*." The whole crew just looked and went "Are you kidding me?" And they were all like "Hey? Is there anything you need? Is everything okay?" [Laughter].

LC: What a cool story! May I ask how old you are?

TJ: How old do you think I am?

LC: Sixty?

TJ: Seventy.

LC: Seventy! Wow!

TJ: I was in *The Young and the Restless* yesterday, and [this guy was] looking at me going, "Dude, I'm retiring at sixty-six! How old are you? Fifty-eight? Fifty-nine? Something like that?" I go, "No, seventy." He says, "Are you kidding me? You're older than I am? You've been on this show . . . you've done all these things. I never knew that!" [Laughter] I look at age as just a number. If you look at it and say "I'm tired," then you're done in this business.

LC: What are some changes you've seen in stunt work over the years?

TJ: What's happened is that all the old stunt guys were very successful and kept everybody safe. All these new guys are coming into the business and they think, *Oh yeah, I can do this.* But they don't really know what they're doing. I teach my kids [Terry has two sons who are professional stuntmen in their own right] and I teach other people: This is what you look out for. You've got to take all the errors that could happen, and you take them out of the equation. A lot of these [new] guys are flying by the seat of their pants. They're like "I can do a take off a motorcycle," then they get jerked off a motorcycle, and they don't put the pick high enough, and they land on their head and they're done. If you don't put your pick high enough—

LC: Your pick?

TJ: Pick point. You got to put it up high so that you come off and down and not just come out and get dragged. It's little things like that that people just don't get. I just got through [coordinating] a thing for this kid. We were hanging him up, and he's doing this dance and stuff, and they have to hook him up just right. People were like "Can't you just do [it this way]?" I said, "No. It's got to be this way." This new director's never dealt with cables before, and he had no idea. They can paint the cables out. I said, "Put as many cables as you want." The CGI guy said, "Yeah, I can paint all those out."

LC: So sometimes you have to advise the director?

TJ: Oh yeah. [One time, a stuntwoman] was getting sick. We had to take her up and spin her around. She was only eighteen or nineteen years old, and she was getting sick. They said, "How about one more take?" I said, "No. We're taking her out right now." They sent a production assistant over and a medic, and they said, "Yeah, she's sick. If we'd have left her up there [it would've been bad]."

LC: How have things changed for stuntwomen?

TJ: They use more women now. Back in the day, we didn't have that many women, so guys would put wigs on. Now these girls are trained, and there are some who are tougher than most guys. This one girl . . . I did a car bit, and I was driving the car, and she got hit and went flying over the car. Then she worked for me four days later on *Days of Our Lives*. We had to do a stair fall. She came, she did it, and she was like "I was a little sore." I said, "I can only imagine."

LC: So you're quite a legend now!

TJ: Sure. I've pretty much got it down to where they have to listen to me. And if they don't, I just walk away. It's my job keeping everybody safe. You've got to know what you're talking about. I've instilled it in my kids. My son was five years old when he started. My oldest started when he was sixteen. He's forty-four now. They're well known [in the world of stunt work]. They'll do a job, and someone will say, "Hey, how's your dad doin'?" And then they'll hire me because I used to do their shows, but now they [my sons] are taking over.

LC: How much longer do you see yourself doing this?

TJ: Until they put me under. [Laughter] I will never give up. If I get to a point where I don't know where I'm at or who I am, then it's a different story.

11

THE COUNTRY BOY WHO MADE GOOD IN LA

Let me say right here and now that I'm a country boy. And, man, I mean the real backwoods!

—Ray Charles

IN THE ICONIC early rock anthem "Johnny B. Goode," Chuck Berry describes a country boy from humble origins who learns to play the guitar really well and whose mother tells him that he'll be the leader of a famous band and that perhaps one day his name will be in lights. One afternoon, I gave a ride to a real-life Johnny B. Goode by the name of Bob Boykin. He didn't have his name in lights, but he went from a backwoods boy from a rural town in Georgia to a successful musician who worked with some of the most famous artists in the fields of country, rock, and studio music for TV and film. When I first met him, I could tell he had an interesting story, so I asked for his contact information, gave him a call a few days later, and got together with him for brunch at a local café.

What follows are some highlights from our interview. Sadly, he passed away a few months later, but he left some fascinating words behind, as you will perhaps agree.

*　　*　　*

LC:　How did you first get into music?

BB:　I got started when I was in the fourth grade, on the trombone and piano lessons. Then one day my dad, who was in the navy, came home for Christmas. I didn't tell him what I wanted for Christmas or anything. After we had Christmas dinner, he said, "Bobby, come out to the car. I want to show you something." He popped the trunk on our Chrysler Imperial, and there was a pawn shop guitar he paid fifteen dollars for as well as an amp. He said that was my Christmas present.

LC:　How old were you?

BB:　I was like ten or twelve. I told him, "You know I can't take that in the house." Grandaddy was against all that kind of stuff, and I didn't want him to know I had it, so we drove the car over to the barn.

LC:　Who was against it?

BB:　My grandfather. He associated it with rock and roll and drugs, and he didn't want me to have anything to do with that kind of stuff.

LC:　I know how in the fifties, the older people were saying that rock and roll was the work of the Devil.

BB:　Yeah, well, we were strict Methodists. We went to church every Sunday. We were devout Christians. Anyway, we drove the car into the barn, and I wrapped the guitar up in a plastic feed bag and stashed it behind the bales of hay and feed. I got a guitar beginner's book at school, and I would play it, and I taught myself.

LC: Are you entirely self-taught, or did somebody at least give you a few pointers?

BB: Well, here's how I put it. I've never taken lessons on guitar. I would meet these guys as I got old enough to start playing, and they would say, "Lemme hear you play. I'm not going to teach you, but we'll jam and play together." That was even better than teaching, because we got really specific on the things I needed to work on. That's how it happened in the early years. So that's how I started. The first bands I was in were high school bands. We played for Saturday night dances at the local schools.

LC: This was in a small town in Georgia?

BB: Yeah. It wasn't even a town. I lived on a dirt road about forty miles outside of Savannah. I had two brothers, and they played in the band. One played piano and one played bass.

LC: When did you get your big break?

BB: I remember it well. I was already playing in clubs. Unbeknownst to my grandparents, [however, because] I never told them what I was doing. They would have forbidden it. I told them I was playing high schools or jamming with my buddies. But I was playing in clubs in Savannah. By the time I was sixteen, I was established around town. People knew me and started hiring me to play in rock and roll bands. I was making a lot of money doing that, and eventually my grandfather found out. But in the beginning, there were artists at this one club I played at on River Street. It was the most happening club on this cobblestone street right on the Savannah River. The river was on one side of the street, and on the other side were all the clubs. That's where the boats came in [in the old days] with the slaves. All the [buildings] that were turned into clubs used to be the housing for the people on the boats. Eventually, they got cleaned up and converted into restaurants. I was playing there every weekend with some major artists, and I would back them up. One was Bobby Womack. The one who really got me was an artist named Sam the Sham. "Woolly Bully" was his big hit. He had several number one hits, and he came through, and I backed him up when I was still in high school. He said, "Hey, boy, you wanna go on the road?" I said, "Yeah!" He said, "The bus is leaving tonight, and we're going to play Daytona for spring break." I went home, threw some clothes together, and got what I needed.

LC: Did you get a chance to say goodbye?

BB: Well, my grandfather heard me come in, and he got up with my grandmother, and they said, "What are you doing? Where you going?" I told them. I'll never forget the look on their faces. They didn't even know I was playing clubs. They found out because my grandfather went through my clothes one night and discovered a big wad of cash. He asked me where I got all that money, and I lied and said that it wasn't all mine and that I had to pay off the other guys in the band after a high school dance. He didn't make too big of a deal about it. Then I said, "I was asked to do a show in Daytona with this guy named Sam the Sham." He said, "Sam who?" I'll never forget the look on his face when he asked, "You know him?" I said, "Well, I've been playing with him for a couple of weekends, and he seems like a nice guy." You know, I've been in touch with him [Sam the Sham] recently. He's a street preacher in Memphis. He helps the homeless.

LC: That's what he's doing now, huh?

BB: Yeah, that's what he does. He's like in his eighties. Anyway, we went and did the show, and after the show that night—my one and only gig was with Sam the Sham, out away from that club [in Savannah] I was playin' at—we did our encore. It was right out on the beach. It was spring break, a lot of bands were playing, and we were the headliners. These guys came up to him, and they were like men in black suits. They grabbed him by the arms and [called Sam by] his real name [Sam Zamudio]. They said, "We're with the FBI, and you're under arrest." I was standing right there. Sam said, "For what?" They said, "Income tax evasion." He'd made millions of dollars off all those hits and never paid any income tax. He turned around and looked at the band and at me and said, "Boys, I guess that was our last gig." He told the bus driver to take us all back to Savannah. The other guys just flew back to wherever they were from. [Years later] I ended up running into him when I was on my first tour in Los Angeles.

LC: What year was that?

BB: 1986.

LC: When you first came to LA?

BB: That was when I first moved here. Very recently [closer to 2019] I met him as a street preacher in Memphis. I walked by, and he was reading a book, but I just had a feeling, so I turned around. He looked up at me, and I knew it was him. He stood up, and he was really tall, and I said, "Is your name Sam the Sham?" He said, "Yeah, it used to be." I said, "I was your guitar player the night you got arrested in Daytona Beach." He laughed and said, "I'll never forget that night!" We talked, and [later] I went in and did the show I was doing. Before that I went out [on the road] with a guy named Dee Clark, same club [in Memphis]. He had two or three big monster hits like "Raindrops" and "Hey Little Girl." I went on the road with him. I did that for about three or four years. The last show I did with him was in Knoxville, Tennessee. I met some guys who were working in Nashville and going back and forth. So I went to Nashville and met Dolly Parton right away and ended up playing with her.

LC: What year was that?

BB: It would have been around 1970 or 1972. I was like nineteen. I went on the road with Dolly and ended up getting a job at the Grand Ole Opry, and Nashville became my home. Then I just stayed in town full time. I got into studio work, getting calls to play on records. Being a studio musician, that's how it started, that part of my life.

LC: Was it mostly country? Was it also rock and roll?

BB: Mostly country, some R & B. I got really good at playing country, even though it wasn't my favorite thing at the time.

LC: Who were some of the artists you played with?

BB: This was before people like Reba McEntire came along, so it was people like Ronnie Milsap, Dolly [Parton], Crystal Gale, Mel Tillis, and that's how I met his daughter, Pam [Tillis], who's a big country artist right now. We've been all over the world together.

LC: My impression is in the mid-1980s, things started to slow down a bit [as far as country], and then you came out to work in movies?

BB: Well, it never slowed down; it's just that I had my fill of it. I wanted to be a composer and play on records and movies and TV shows that I wanted to do, instead of just getting calls from the union and being a hired gun—that's the life of a studio musician. I had this other passion, composing. I started doing Saturday morning cartoons for Marvel Comics, like *Spider-Man* and *Batman*. I was playing guitar.

LC: Those are pretty big franchises now as movies.

BB: Now it's a different world. The whole studio scene is drying up. The real money now is in film and TV. It's all downloads. We're all struggling to get paid.

LC: I notice a lot of acts [artists] from a long time ago are going back on the road.

BB: The reason is that the tickets sales are good, but you also sell more merchandise. It's a big business. I did a lot of that, too, when I was younger. It could be very difficult and challenging physically. You can get really beat up, physically, not enough rest, overbooked, and trying to get to the show.

LC: I remember we were talking about how a lot of artists, like Tom Petty, Michael Jackson, Prince—

BB: That's why they all got hooked on those sleeping pills, because they book you so tight that you just don't have time to rest, and you have to get up and go. Actors, too, have that same problem. That's how Heath Ledger died. He was complaining about how he had to get up at four in the morning and be on set. He wouldn't get back to his hotel until midnight or one. After days and days of that, you'll do anything to get to sleep. Then he overdid it one night, and that's what happened.

LC: I remember we were talking about Tom Petty and how, after a live show, you're so keyed up it's hard to . . . I guess drugs helped him to—

BB: Yeah, to wind down. I've been there. I've never done the drugs, but I've been there. Maybe a little of my grandfather rubbed off on me. I always heard his voice in the back of my mind. That's what he was so worried about. I was around it, but I was always free [from it].

LC: I know a lot of artists are into the illegal drugs, but I'm thinking even the ones that are prescribed.

BB: They all were doing the same stuff. They were taking the opioids by prescription and the fentanyl, which will put you to sleep when you have an operation. And they put it in combination, but if you take too much of it, it's deadly. That's what happened to Michael Jackson.

LC: I wanted to ask about your trip across the country with John Schneider.

BB: That would have been around 1989 or 1990. He had just finished a play on Broadway called *Grand Hotel.* He was the lead. They had just closed, and he had had enough of the city life and hotel rooms. He had a big Harley-Davidson roadster. This thing was huge, and it had a back seat on it as big as this chair I'm sittin' in. So we had that on a trailer, and he bought some kind of old station wagon. The way it went down was he called me up. It was like a Saturday night, and he said, "Hey, Bobby. What're you doing?" I was on a date. We had just had dinner and were watching TV. He said, "There's a ticket waiting for you at the airport. Why don't you meet me?" It was some little town right outside of New York. So I flew there in the middle of the night. John drove the station wagon and the Harley to that airport, and we took the Harley, and he flew out another of his assistants. When he and I took the Harley, his assistant would drive the station wagon and the trailer. We would write songs. We rode into buffalo herds. I don't remember what it's called, but it's the northern version of Route 66, and it goes from [the] East Coast to [the] West Coast, just below the Canadian border. There are tons of little towns along that strip, and they're all like ghost towns now. There used to be heavy business when there were trains. So we took that route and went all the way across the country. We stayed in tiny towns and motels. And sometimes we'd ride out into the country.

LC: Did people recognize him?

BB: Oh yeah, everywhere! He's very gracious about that, but it gets to be a little overbearing sometimes. We couldn't go into any restaurant; people always knew. But that was a lot of fun. We'd be driving along in the car at night, and he'd say, "Bobby, tell me some of those stories." We'd stop and write songs, and I remember in Wyoming that we saw a buffalo herd. We rode out and spent the night with them, out in the middle of a field. Then we'd get our guitars out and write some songs. That's how that happened.

LC: After you came to LA, how did you get into movies?

BB: I played guitar on some TV shows, and I got to meet a lot of the composers and music supervisors, which is totally different from the people who do records. It's two separate businesses. The last place I lived in Nashville was on Mel Tillis's farm. I lived in one house, and Emmylou Harris was like two hundred feet away from me, and she lived in the other house. What's funny is that when I had moved to LA, one of the studios I worked at was owned by a guy named Brian Ahern, and he was married to Emmylou Harris. They had just gotten divorced [in 1984], but it wasn't like a real messy divorce. They were still friends. [Ahern continued to produce albums for Emmylou Harris well into the twenty-first century.] I was working in that studio. I think it was [for] Billy Idol.

LC: Billy Idol, the punk rock guy?

BB: Yeah, it was one of those jobs [where] I got called, and I didn't know who I was going to be playing with until I got there. Most of the time, you never know until you show up. It could be anything or anybody. So I was working, and I saw Emmylou Harris in the office, and Emmylou was talking with Brian Ahern. It's funny how things worked out. I think God had a lot to do with me being in the right place at the right time. So Emmylou had left, and I told Brian that I used to live next to her. We talked about what I had been doing. He had produced so many big records, like Linda Ronstadt and James Taylor. So anyway, I met his secretary that day, and she heard the whole conversation, and for some reason, she liked me, and she said,

"You know, my husband is the senior vice president of Sony Music, for all the TV shows and films." I told them that I had written a lot of songs for Crystal Gale, and I said part of the reason for moving to LA was that I wanted to get into the composing scene, so I had the background. I'd never done it, but I knew I could. I met her husband [the Sony Music senior vice president], and he took me under his wing, and he called me up one day. The first day it was a cattle call where every composer who worked for Sony got the same script and the same call to write a song for a show called *Married with Children*. It was the number one show on TV at the time; they had just recorded a hundred episodes. So they had a big blowout in a restaurant in Beverly Hills, and they wanted a song for the occasion. I guess forty different composers wrote for that. I remember going into his office, and there was a cardboard box with cassettes; he said those were the ones that just came in. So I learned a long time ago to turn mine in at the end. I wrote a hip-hop song, and I gave [it] to him. I got a phone call the next day, and they said, "Your song's the one they picked."

LC: So if I wanted to find the episode, where I could hear it?

BB: It was never on an episode; it was just for that one occasion. They had a live hip-hop band, they hired an artist named John Lewis [not to be confused with the Congressman with the same name]. It was just for their awards show. Anyway, that led to him [the Sony executive] starting to call me for other shows. When they had corporate shows [parties] for Sony, I was the go-to guy, and it turned out to be really successful. Then a show came along, and he called me and said, "I'm submitting you as the composer, but you got to write for a new show that's coming up. It's called *Married People*." *Married with Children* was still on the air, but it was only reruns, so this was a totally different script and storyline. I had to come up with a theme for *Married People* that was appropriate for what that show was about. So I wrote a song, and about twenty other guys wrote songs, too. And again, mine got picked as the theme. They bought it, and they hired me. Then [they asked] who was going to do the music for the episodes during the week. This guy went to the president of Sony and said, "This guy, he's never done it before, but I'm going to back him up. I think he can do it, and we should give him a chance." That's a lot of responsibility; you got to deliver on time, every week, no exceptions, because the show has to be aired, and they have to put it into the show. You've got to do what's called a work for hire contract and a union contract for the music part of it, so two contracts. I had to deliver. Sometimes I wouldn't even get the script for the new show. We would have these casting meetings. The show aired on Wednesday nights, and sometimes the Friday before that Wednesday, we would have what was called a spotting session or a cast meeting, where the director [would] tell me what her vision is or what the storyline was about—whether they wanted up-tempo or sad or happy or whatever. I had the weekend to write it, and on Monday I was supposed to deliver it. Basically, I got a credit card from Sony [and was told to] go into any studio I wanted, hire any musicians I wanted—it didn't matter what it cost—just be on time. I did twenty-two shows, and I did not have to rewrite one note of anything I did.

LC: Is the show [*Married People*] something you can find online?

BB: Yeah, you can find it. We were number one in our time slot in prime time on ABC, and the directors and producers of that show were working on another side project that nobody knew about. They knew that after twenty-two episodes, their contract would have to be renegotiated or canceled. They asked for more than double in their renegotiation of the contract. We were number one in the time slot, and the network wanted to keep it going, but they wouldn't pay that much.

LC: Because they were already working on something else?

BB: They wanted to bomb their own show so that they could get this new show off the ground. And guess what the new show was called?

LC: That's what I was wondering.

BB: *The Nanny* with Fran Drescher. That was the new show. And the funny thing was, they offered me that show, and I turned it down. I just wasn't into the storyline. *Married People* was mostly live musicians. *The Nanny* had a guy with one synthesizer, like *Seinfeld,* and I didn't want to do that. So I said no. I could have retired with a few million more than I have now. That [show] was very successful and ran [for] several years. That's the inside stuff that happens in Hollywood that nobody knows.

LC: So after *Married People* got canceled, what was next for you?

BB: I continued doing studio work. I wrote a lot of music for *Sex in the City.* I do work for hire, where I get calls from Sony or a music supervisor who I met in the studio somewhere to write a song for a specific scene. I did a lot of different shows, and I still get royalty checks from some of that work.

BB: I had a friend who wrote "Wind beneath My Wings." It's like the number one wedding song of all time. It's considered a classic, like big money, millions of dollars from one song. But he continued to write, and he has a big house up in Studio City. I was watching the Super Bowl with him—I think it was in the nineties—and a song came on, and it was his song they played on one of the commercials during the Super Bowl. But they didn't get permission. You have to do what's called a performance license with the owners of the music. In his case, it was Warner Brothers; that was his publisher. So he heard it, and because they could track it—it was the Super Bowl—he got a six-figure check. I'm dealing with that right now. Ever watch a show called *Little Big Lies*?

LC: I've heard of it, but I haven't watched it.

BB: It's the number one show on HBO, other than *Game of Thrones*, but that's gone. This is still going. It's got Nicole Kidman, Reese Witherspoon, Meryl Streep. I've got two or three songs in different episodes, where they just play, like, thirty seconds or a minute. The season finale just aired about three weeks ago. In the final episode, Christina [Vierra] and I had recorded a track. She sounds just like Janis Joplin. The producer said, "We want to close our season out with her." They loved her voice so much. So we recorded it. I put the band together. And they used it without contacting our publisher, Universal. They're the biggest publisher in the world, so you can't really pull something like that with them. We only found out because we were both getting tons of phone calls from friends who had seen the show, and they knew her voice and knew that we had done it. But they didn't have a license, so my lawyers are filing a lawsuit right now. They've already made a soundtrack album they're selling without permission. It's all over Amazon and anywhere you can buy music for download. My lawyer drafted a cease and desist letter and demanded that they cough up some major bucks. But they've got so much money, they don't care. I've seen a lot in this town. A big studio like that, they don't care.

LC: I wanted to ask about your friend who played with Doc Severinsen.

BB: Oh yeah, Ernie Watts. I just talked to him. He's usually out of the country most of the time, on tour somewhere. He's got places in Indonesia, Japan, Europe. Doc lives in Monterrey, Mexico, but he still does tours. He [Ernie Watts] was really the reason I got, sort of, pushed to the front of the line for gigs when I first came to town. People found out that I was working with him, and he was recommending me for gigs, and there were no questions asked. I met him in Kenny Rogers's studio. I was living in Nashville, and I came out here [to LA] to play on Kenny Rogers's record, and Ernie was in the horn section. There was a show called *Star Search*. I wrote a song that they wanted really badly. The song was called "The Other Side of Nashville." It was used in a commercial to promote music in Nashville that wasn't country. It was like, we're not just whistling Dixie down here, and I played some licks like the Stones or Zeppelin. They liked it, and they put it on the radio and TV. We performed it live. Pam Tillis and I wrote it, and Pam sang it. So it wasn't really a band; it was just some friends of mine. We were all studio musicians. We formed a band just for that one song and recorded it. Everybody was doing really well and wasn't too interested in being on *Star Search*. I got phone calls, and I politely declined. One day, I'm in a session in Nashville, and I see guys in suits in the control room. The engineer comes over and says, "Bobby, when we're done with this track, there are some guys who want to talk to you." We finished playing, and I went in there, and they said, "We just flew out here from Los Angeles to try to persuade you to do *Star Search*. What will it take?" They wanted that song that badly [that] they flew out two guys with a checkbook. I told them I didn't have a band, so I looked at the guys I was playing with that morning—it was a jingle thing with Amy Grant—and I said, "Y'all ever been to LA?" They said no. I asked, "You wanna go?" That's how it came together.

LC: That became your band, huh?

BB: That became my band. I wanted to put horns on that song, and I went back into Kenny Rogers's studio because I knew those guys. I called Ernie [Watts], and he had just gotten off the road with the Rolling Stones. He was worn out, hadn't slept for days, just got off the plane. But he did it for me. That was another one of those God moments for me that put us in each other's lives at the right time. We did the *Star Search* thing, and we would have won, but I didn't want to win because we didn't have a band or anything. The band we were up against is now a very successful band called Sawyer Brown. We ended up tying with them. I'd been playing on Sawyer Brown's tracks. I don't know how they found out that I played on the music that I was competing against, but they got voted as the winners. I was disqualified. That was my second trip to LA, and I loved it so much, I went home and called some friends who were guitar players and farmed out the work to them and then started packing. I got on a plane, and I didn't have a car or anything when I first got here. I took the bus to a couple of gigs. Then I knew I loved it, and I got a place here in Studio City. I lived there fourteen years.

LC: Was that with your roommate, Ernie?

BB: Yeah, Ernie Watts. I came out here, and I met Ernie. He was doing the *Tonight Show.* He did that show for thirty-two years. And then Doc [Severinsen] said, "Just take a little time off and come in whenever you're in town and you want to do it. When you don't want to do it, I'll get somebody else." He didn't need the money, so he was focusing more on his career as a solo artist, and so that's why he left the *Tonight Show.* He's one of the most recorded session horn players. The guitar player who was in that band was named Bob Bain. Before the *Tonight Show* and during the early *Tonight Show* years, he played the Peter Gunn theme and some of the most classic guitar themes [in film and TV] to this day, like *Batman* and *Pink Panther* and all of Henry Mancini's work. That was all him. Ernie did a lot of appearances live with orchestras, too. Henry Mancini used to bring Ernie out on the road for those things. But this guy, Bob Bain, I used to hang out with him after the shows, and I had no idea he had done all that. That's how it is for studio musicians; they're in the background. They're the guys playing the music that you hear, but you don't know who they are. Glen Campbell was like that.

LC: The guy who sang "Rhinestone Cowboy" in the seventies?

BB: Yeah. Before he became a solo artist, he was a studio musician. [Bob mentioned Toto as well as a group of studio musicians who made it big with an album that contained their hits "Africa" and "Rosanna."] It's like the Beach Boys. They [studio musicians] played on a lot of the Beach Boys hits. A woman bass player named Carol Kaye did all those great surfing bass lines, and she played for Sonny and Cher's "The Beat Goes On." That would have been the best time of any to be a studio player.

*　　*　　*

Bob Boykin passed away a few months after this interview, on February 22, 2020. Thanks for the music, Bob, and requiescat in pace. Here's hoping the beat goes on and that you're playing happily in heaven.

12

LATINO RIDERS AND A TALK WITH LOUIS PEREZ OF LOS LOBOS

Our roots will always be in Mexico, deep down in that rich soil

—Oscar Zeta Acosta

DRIVING FOR LYFT, one meets people from various levels of society: working-class employees of restaurants and retail stores, college kids, graphic designers, corporate executives, and celebrities and the people who work with them. Sometimes there are people who belong to more than one class. One gentleman was on his way to a night shift at Target, but in his home country (he told me in

Spanish), he had been a university professor. He took the job at Target because he couldn't speak English, and it was the best job he could get since arriving in Los Angeles.

Another gentleman I picked up in West Hollywood was on his way to his home in Huntington Park. He had grown up in Mexico City and was now working as a physical therapist. He had studied hard to earn a doctor of physical therapy degree but had not had the time or inclination to master English. When I told him about my day job as an English teacher, he groaned, then laughed and said, "English! That was my worst subject." After I said that I don't have to be an English teacher while driving for Lyft, we had a very pleasant conversation. I told him about my visit to Mexico City several years ago and how impressed I was by the cleanliness of the subways there. I said it was probably the cleanest subway system I had seen in a big city—even cleaner than subways in London and Paris. He also described some of his challenges as a physical therapist: how some people need to understand that they cannot improve their condition if they don't put in the time to exercise. We shared a laugh when we realized that we both give homework and have to deal with those who don't complete it.

After I dropped him off, I picked up a young woman named Rosa, who was meeting up with some friends to go out to a comedy club. I asked if she had ever been to a comedy club before, and she said she hadn't. I told her I didn't think I had either, but I went to a lot of concerts in the eighties and nineties. I asked if she had ever heard of a band called Los Lobos from East LA. She said she hadn't and asked what their most famous song was.

I replied, "Have you seen the movie *La Bamba* about the life of Ritchie Valens?" She answered that she had. I said, "They did the soundtrack for that film. Also, they had a cameo in the scene where Ritchie's brother Bob takes him to a bar in Tijuana, and there's a live band playing traditional Mexican instruments. The band that Ritchie first hears playing 'La Bamba' was Los Lobos."

She said, "Oh, that's them, huh? I'll have to check out their music."

I told her that classic rock stations still play the Los Lobos version of "La Bamba" once in a while, but the song that I remember hearing the most in the 1980s was "How Will the Wolf Survive?" which, I told her, was actually about the Latino people. After a pause, I continued. "All this land we're on now was once Mexico." One of the ironies of history is that before 1848, all the illegal immigrants in California spoke English.

I mentioned to Rosa that the guy who wrote that song, Louis Perez, had told me about the songs he wrote when I interviewed him many years ago. Before I became a teacher, I did a brief stint as a writer for a Catholic youth magazine. One of the coolest things I got to do was interview the main songwriter for the band, and he said some really cool things about growing up Latino in East LA and about the rock bands of the LA club scene during the 1980s.

Because most of the interview with Louis Perez was not published, here are some excerpts from it, published for the first time. Rosa, if you ever read this, I hope you enjoy it. It's a fuller version of the parts I mentioned to you when we talked.

*   *   *

LC: People have come to identify Los Lobos with integrity of style and traditional values of God and family. You were in *Time* magazine, you played with Paul Simon, and "La Bamba" still gets played on VH1 and MTV.

LP: Yeah, right. I think MTV did burn out with that.

LC: With all the success, is it a struggle to hold on to good values?

LP: Well, we've been together for seventeen years [this was in 1990]. We were together as a group since 1974, and we had been together for ten or eleven years before we got [a] legitimate recording contract.

LC: I understand you were mostly playing confirmations and weddings?

LP: Yeah. The way we usually put it is if you're a Mexican American and got married between 1974 and 1980, we probably did your wedding.

LC: Did you go to Roosevelt?

LP: Garfield. James E. Garfield High School. That's a rival school, man.

LC: Oh, sorry.

LP: [Laughter] We went to Garfield High School together, and we all knew each other. We were all musicians, but we didn't play together [at first]. David [Hidalgo] and Cesar [Rosas] went to the same junior high together, even though they ran in different circles. Conrad [Lozano] and I lived in the same neighborhood. We didn't really hang out together, but we knew each other, and I kind of got closer to David in the last years of high school. Right out of high school, David and I formed a band, and Cesar had his band, and Conrad had his band, and we started getting together, just as friends. This band [Los Lobos] formed as a sort of departure from our usual bands. [The other bands] would want me to get into clubs, but to play in the clubs, you have to make popular music. The music we enjoyed playing was just obscure cover songs off [our] favorite records.

LC: You're supposed to do your own stuff at some point. I mean, I never heard of a band that made it big doing just cover stuff.

LP: Yeah, right. We got bored doing all the cover stuff, and we started moonlighting and hanging out.

LC: Like the LA club scene?

LP: No, you're getting way ahead. This was like 1974. We started this band out of just wanting to do something completely different. At that time, it was unheard of—young people playing Mexican music. We all went through the process of trying to deny our ethnic background. Like any kid growing up in America tries to be an American. But somehow we found ourselves, at a young age, back to Mexican music and drew a great deal of satisfaction from that. Young people slowly came around and got interested in what we were doing. In the early 1970s, the whole Chicano renaissance thing [started], with Mexican American study groups in colleges, and this group continued as just a working band [that became] sort of a fixture in the East LA Mexican community. At that point, it was all acoustic music, nothing electric, and there was regional music from different parts of Mexico, so we were a folkloric kind of outfit.

LC: How did you get into rock and roll?

LP: Finally, toward the end of the seventies, out of desperation, we were playing these really horrible kind of gigs, and we felt in a rut, not going anywhere, and at that point the new music scene was happening in Hollywood, and Dave and I would find ourselves traveling over to that side of town and checking out bands like the Blasters and X and a lot of the new bands that were considered the new music.

LC: This was about the time that Van Halen got their start and the Go-Gos.

LP: Yeah, absolutely. We would run into them regularly: X, the Go-Gos, the Blasters—a lot of different bands. It was a really good thing for us: We finally, as a group, made that transition. We packed up the old Dodge van and went across the LA River to Hollywood and started to play the local clubs and got to know the Blasters. They helped us out by inviting us to open shows for them. It wasn't very long before we were pretty much welcome into the scene. We continued playing that scene until we finally picked up a lot of local critics who were writing about the band, and we ended up with a deal and recorded our first record in 1983 called *A Time to Dance*.

LC: That was your first one, huh?

LP: That was the very first one. We went out on the road for the first time. We were all Southern California kids who had never been anywhere, and all of a sudden, we're in the middle of Burlington, Vermont, or Buffalo, New York, or something. But to get back to your question about how we maintain our family ethic in a business like this: We were together for many, many years as friends, and our families have been with us since the very beginning, so all of us sacrificed a great deal, [for example, time with] spouses and children, through all the early years when we really felt that we were doing something special and [that] we had to hang on to this dream. The perseverance and our faith paid off; we've enjoyed some success. We owe a lot to our family and friends and, really, the fact that we have been together and [that] we've all hung together through tough times. The way we perceive success is a lot different from a band that was together for seventeen months; we've been together for seventeen years. Before our hits started spinning, we were pretty much grounded, and we have a secure family foundation.

LC: Are you all married?

LP: Yeah, we're all married, and we all have children. It's family, and friends, and being together for that long [that] sort of tempers the way we perceive success and the big picture.

LC: That's great. So you don't get into hard-core infighting like other groups [that are always breaking up and changing personnel]? It doesn't seem that way with Los Lobos.

LP: No, we couldn't. [Laughter] After you've been together for this long, it's almost like a marriage. We're like one big family. I can't imagine getting along without seeing these guys; I mean, we're just like brothers. You know, the fact that I became a drummer was because [I played guitar all my life], but I started playing drums out of necessity because . . .

LC: You needed a drummer.

LP: Yeah. We started to play Tex-Mex music, and David learned the accordion. We couldn't see just putting out a classified ad for an accordion player or a drummer; we just made them.

LC: Could you give me a rundown of what each guy plays?

LP: David is the most versatile. He plays violin and accordion and guitars and a lot of different string instruments. The same goes for the rest of us. Cesar plays *bajocesto*, which is a Mexican instrument that developed out of the border area of Texas and Mexico. He [also plays] other string instruments [that are] regional instruments of Mexico because they vary. I do the same: I play drums, and I play guitar, and [I play] a lot of these more exotic-type instruments that come from Mexico. [Los Lobos can be seen playing Mexican instruments in their cameo scene in the hit 1987 film *La Bamba*, about the life of Ritchie Valens. They are the band in the cantina in Tijuana that plays "La Bamba" when Ritchie first gets inspired to record his own version.]

LC: What are some of the exotic instruments you guys play?

LP: In Mexico, from region to region, it varies as far as instruments go. I play these instruments from Veracruz, like one called the jarana. David plays one that's called the *requinto jarocho*. Conrad, our bass player, plays electric bass and upright bass, and he also plays a big Mexican bass, which is called a *guitarron*. That's the one you see in mariachi groups.

LC: I think that's what makes people admire you—you're yourselves, and you have so much to offer.

LP: I like to say that whenever we needed something, we've been friends for too long to think about bringing in someone else—even though we did [once]. We brought in Steve Berlin. It seems like Steve was just one of the bunch. It happened when we were playing the LA club scene. He came and hung out, and he was willing to go through all the hard knocks of coming up through the scene in Hollywood and hanging out with us in the garage, working on material and hitting the taco trucks at 4:00 a.m. after a gig at Wong's in Chinatown. [Laughter] So he pretty much came one day and never left.

LC: That's great. When did you guys get the name Los Lobos?

LP: The way that happened is there are a lot of groups around that play Tex-Mex music that are called the Hurricanes or the Tigers or the Wolves. There are a lot of these names floating around, and there's one group that's called Los Lobos del Norte [The Wolves of the North]. So we decided to call ourselves Los Lobos del Este [The Wolves of the East] because we were from East LA, so it was kind of a joke. Little did we know, it would almost become a symbolic thing when we came onto the scene. People couldn't figure out what we were about. This band plays Mexican music in Spanish and old rock and roll music and original songs that fall somewhere in between. It was during that time that the name Los Lobos actually took on a different meaning—like the creature that was misunderstood. That's pretty much the theme of our first LP: "How Will the Wolf Survive?" That particular song—

LC: That was a song that really took off for you.

LP: Yeah, it really broke a lot of ground for us. It was ranked really high on the top ten list from coast to coast. That was the year we got Band of the Year from *Rolling Stone* and the number three record of the year and all kinds of accolades. We were just a little band that had devoted all our energy to something we really believed in, and then all of this was happening.

LC: Was there ever a time when you felt a conflict between your family obligations and your music?

LP: There were times I used to say, "I just got to throw this dream away and go about the business of providing for my family."

Those were the times I felt a direct conflict. It takes a great deal of effort to maintain a family ethic and do this kind of business. But I find that when I come through the door [of home] after touring, I become Dad, and I get my little boys who run around, and I go from the rock and roll guy to just a father of three boys and a husband to a very devout and loving wife. I thank God for providing me with those things that keep everything in the right perspective. Because [in] this business, you can easily get swayed into thinking you're something else. I remember coming back from the Grammys. We won a Grammy for *La Pistola y El Corazón*, our Spanish-language album. I walked in the door, and my mother-in-law stood there—she had been babysitting—and she looked at me and said, "Hey, [there are] no more diapers!" [Laughter] Suddenly, you're jolted back into reality, you know? There we were going to the local all-night market to pick up a package of diapers!

LC: Right after a Grammy [win]!

LP: Yeah, I'm tellin' you! God has a way of having some sort of circuit breaker that kind of just reminds you that before you start thinking you're too cool, here's a little bit of reality. [Laughter]

LC: Whose idea was it to have the picture of Our Lady of Guadalupe on the big bass drum?

LP: Oh, that's mine. She's my American Express card: you don't leave home without her! [Laughter]

LC: [Laughter] So is God important to Los Lobos?

LP: We all have faith in God. Some of us are just a little more devout than others. I think as we get older, we want to hang on to certain values we had when we were young. I know I went through a period as an adolescent when I didn't want to have anything to do with being a Mexican American. I went through a period of wanting to deny my culture and everything that went with it. But as we get older, we find ourselves realizing that the things your parents try to give you, that you've tried your best to throw away, somehow stay with you. You go back and you realize that this stuff was really important. I think success has done something to us to actually bring us closer to God. Because success is kind of frightening; it does something to you where you feel like you need to hang on to something. Your identity is almost . . .

LC: Lost?

LP: Yeah. *La Bamba* was like this huge megahit all over the world, man, and it was scary. We found ourselves getting back together and asking, "What are we doing?" When we tried to find ourselves again, I came up with that record of Mexican music, which was a very unlikely move for a band after a big number one hit—to come back with something that was as ethnic as that. Everybody thought we'd come back with *La Bamba II* or something, but we did the opposite. We tried to do something that meant more. We took the attention and the success and tried to use it in a positive way—to embrace our culture.

LC: Here's a question about the title song on your album *The Neighborhood* [released in 1990]. The song "The Neighborhood" paints a resilient portrait of a poor family desperately struggling to survive but still thankful to God.

LP: I tried to paint this portrait to address the issue of drugs and violence in the inner city. We're saying that at a time when peace has become almost a meaningless word, that it still means something. Peace is something we really need now more than ever.

LC: I guess the neighborhood could be the whole world.

LP: Exactly; that's the next thing I was going to say. It's speaking to a world community. It talks about a particular problem, but in the chorus, I think we're addressing a world neighborhood. Peace is something we all need. Inner peace is something we need to find within ourselves and bring peace to the rest of the world. It's a very idealistic statement, but it's something I really believe in. I believe that, as children, we're very unaffected and pure, and as we get older, we develop this kind of armor, or shield, that kind of protects us from everything. But sometimes a little bit of our soul leaks out, and that's when we write, when we make pictures, and when we can love.

LC: It's like a little child's voice saying, "Why can't everybody just get along?"

LP: Yeah. It's a very vulnerable way of looking at things, but in vulnerability, we're able to say that we need each other. We need to remember that we're all the same in the eyes of God, whatever our color or whatever [our beliefs]. I've never been one who would want to put down other faiths; it's the way that they interpret God for themselves, in their own lives and through their own cultures. We all need to understand that before we can even start a dialogue.

LC: Last question: Los Lobos frankly amazes me. You guys are so authentically yourselves. You don't try to get all weird or become something you're not in order to sell your records, and yet you're successful. You don't bend over backward to court popularity, but you're still popular. How do you get away with it?

LP: When we started playing our music, we said, "Look, there's no question that there are four Mexican American people onstage. There's no question that the name of the band is Spanish." We never tried to pass ourselves off as anything else. [Going] back to what I said about vulnerability, when you can show people exactly who you are and what you're trying to do, I think people say, "Hey, this is a breath of fresh air in a business that's all about glitz and packaging." This is what we are. There's nothing more to us. This is the music that we write, and these songs are about things we really believe in. That's how we get away with it. People admire us for being honest. I guess we *do* get away with it!

13

WHO IS CHARLES LUMMIS? AN INTERVIEW WITH RANGER CHRISTIAN RODRIGUEZ

*"Are there not railroads . . . enough, that you must walk?"
That is what a great many of my friends said when they
learned of my determination to travel from Ohio to
California on foot.*

—Charles Lummis

ONE DAY MY passenger was Christian Rodriguez, whom I recognized from one of my visits to El Alisal, the stone house of Charles

Lummis that was built between 1897 and 1910 and that still stands in the Arroyo Seco neighborhood of Northeast Los Angeles. Christian Rodriguez is the curator and docent at El Alisal who gave a captivating presentation to the group of teachers I brought to visit the historic site where Lummis once lived. Christian also appears in documentaries on the history of Southern California, such as the PBS documentary *Larger Than Life: Charles Fletcher Lummis* and the KCET documentary *Charles Lummis: Reimagining the American West*. Lummis was a pretty important dude in the story of Los Angeles, and Christian Rodriguez was kind enough to sit down with me to talk about why as well as share his own experiences.

Charles Lummis (1859–1928), one of the most important of LA preservationists.

Ranger Christian Rodriguez talking to teachers at the Lummis House, El Alisal, in Arroyo Seco, Northeast LA.

*　　*　　*

LC:　When or how did you start at the Lummis House?

CR:　It's interesting, because I don't have a history background. It has just been an interest of mine. I had a nine-to-five job doing internet marketing up until 2011. It was fine, but I wasn't passionate about it or anything. I quit that job impetuously;

there was no reason for me to quit. It was just time for me to move on.

LC: You'd had enough.

CR: Yeah, I'd had enough. I just thought, *It's time to move on to something else.* But then that something else didn't come around for like half a year, and then they asked me to come back. I ended up going back to that company, working for like another year and a half. Then I quit a second time. But in between that time that I wasn't working, I was living in Highland Park, just down the street from the Lummis House.

LC: Did you grow up in the Arroyo Seco area?

CR: No. I grew up in the South Bay.

LC: Me, too!

CR: Where?

LC: Torrance. You?

CR: I grew up in Hawthorne, by El Camino College.

LC: I went to El Camino for a year and a half. There's a Domino's Pizza across the street from the campus.

CR: Oh yeah, on Crenshaw.

LC: I worked at that Domino's.

CR: Where in Torrance did you grow up?

LC: Near the corner of Anza and Pacific Coast Highway.

CR: I know where that is. So you went to [Torrance] South High School.

LC: I graduated from South High, yeah.

CR: I grew up in the South Bay, and I lived there until about 2009 or 2010. Then I moved up here [Arroyo Seco, just north of downtown LA] because of that e-commerce job. I lived most of my life in Los Angeles, without a car—on purpose. When I moved up closer to LA, I wanted to be nearer to a public transit line, so I moved to Highland Park. At that time, Highland Park was really inexpensive. It was only just beginning to gentrify.

Rent was cheap. It was one of the last vestiges of cheap rent by a transit line. So I had quit my job, and I was trying to look for a job, but it wasn't happening. I'm one of those people who believes I'm better when I'm busier. I thought, *I'll go volunteer and do something that I enjoy.* So I'm in Highland Park, and I knew all these historic sites, and I had never been to any of them. I had been to the Southwest Museum on a field trip. But the Southwest Museum at that time was still closed. I knew vaguely of the Charles Lummis House; I knew what it was. And I knew about the Heritage Square Museum. So I started volunteering at the Heritage Square Museum. I happened to go there, and I inquired about volunteering, and they were like "Oh, the volunteer training is starting next week." I went to the volunteer training. The first weekend of volunteer train-ing, I'm on my way back to my house when I walked past the Lummis House, and it was open. I was like "Oh, I haven't seen this one yet," and I went inside. All I remember of my first impression of the place was that it wasn't what I'd imagined. I knew it was part of the craftsman movement and that it was a stone house. I didn't know much else.

LC: You didn't know much about Charles Lummis?

CR: No. I don't even know if I knew he was the founder of the Southwest Museum at that point. I just knew that this was a rustic craftsman house and that it was built by hand; it was made of stone. For whatever reason, when I went there, it was something completely different from what I imagined. There was something that struck me about the place as very *accessible.* People come in on weekends, [and] I get this virtually every weekend: "Oh! I could live here!" It contrasts with the Victorian houses [of Heritage Square]. It's like "This is neat, but I would never want to live here."

LC: I see.

CR: At that time, the Charles Lummis House was the home of the Historical Society of Southern California, [which had been] based at the Lummis House for fifty years, starting in 1965. In 2011, I started volunteering for the historical society. I was trying to find another job for six months. I was becoming desperate, then my old company called me, and they were like "Oh, you want to come back? We'll have you back!" So I went to the historical society [curator] and said, "I'm going to be working a nine-to-five [job]," because I was [volunteering at the historical society] every day. I felt bad because I met lovely people, and I got excellent training at [the] Heritage Square Museum. I ended up completing the training, and I think I did two tours there. Then I ended up just falling in love with the Charles Lummis House.

LC: They were both only volunteer gigs, right?

CR: When the historical society was there, [the Lummis House] had staff. They had a curator, and they had a couple [of] other part-time staff people. But the Historical Society of Southern California also does other things. They did, and continue to do, other things besides run that museum. They publish a journal, *The Southern California Quarterly*, which is one of the more important scholarly journals, at least on Southern California history. They've been publishing that since 1883. It's the second longest continuous publication behind the *Los Angeles Times*, and they still publish [it].

LC: Lummis was involved in both, right?

CR: Lummis was a member of the historical society. The Historical Society of Southern California predates Lummis's walk to Southern California. [Lummis left Cincinnati on September 12, 1884, and arrived in Los Angeles on February 1, 1885.] I went back to the historical society and said, "I'm working again. I still want to volunteer here, because I really enjoy coming here and giving tours, but I can't be here every day anymore." The next week, the curator of the society spoke to the executive director and [said], "What if we pay you?" They liked me enough that [they said], "We kind of want you here at least on Saturdays and Sundays." I said, "Well, if you pay me . . ."

LC: If you twist my arm?

CR: Right, if you twist my arm! [Laughter] Then I did other projects for them. I helped them with marketing stuff, because that was my area: email lists, social media, that kind of stuff. That's how I got started at the Charles Lummis House when the Historical Society of Southern California was still there. Then, ultimately, they left. They had an operating agreement with the city [of Los Angeles].

LC: So is it now [run by] the city then?

CR: Correct.

LC: Is it the Department of Parks and Recreation?

CR: Yes. The city owns the house. Charles Lummis gave the house to the Southwest Museum when he died in 1928. But he didn't give them an endowment to turn the house into a museum. So they let the family continue to live there, like caretakers, and they acquired his collection. That's why all of Lummis's ethnographic [mostly Native American] and his papers are part of the Southwest Museum. Because he gave it all to them, the house included; he intended to turn the house into a museum. Then there was a big preservation battle [to preserve the house] in the 1930s. I'm pretty sure it's connected to the design and construction of the parkway. [The Arroyo Seco Parkway, the first freeway completed in California, runs between downtown Los Angeles and Pasadena.]

LC: Oh yeah. It was finished in 1939.

CR: Correct. I've never read anywhere that there was an explicit threat or [that] they said, "Oh, we're going to tear down the house to build this parkway." But, clearly, it seems like that's what people were worked up about, because the push to preserve the house as a museum is in the mid- to late 1930s. It was mostly the League of Women Voters, but then there was a group formed called the Lummis Memorial Association. Althea Warren, who was the head of the Los Angeles Public Library, led it.

LC: I've heard that name.

CR: Have you read the Susan Orlean book *The Library Book*?

LC: No. [I hadn't read it at the time, but I did read it in 2023.]

CR: It's about the history of the Los Angeles Public Library, and there's a whole thing in there about Althea Warren. She was the head of the LA Public Library, and she was a mentor to Lawrence Clark Powell [who was later the university librarian at UCLA and, after moving to Arizona in 1971, was instrumental in the development of the University of Arizona Graduate School of Library Science].

CR: Anyway, they built the [Arroyo Seco] Parkway. Then the Southwest Museum sold the house to the state [of California] in 1943. Since 1943, the Charles Lummis House doesn't have an institutional connection to the Southwest Museum anymore. But for whatever reason, the state had the city manage it. The state owned it, but the city [Department of Recreation and Parks] was managing the property. Then, eventually, after the historical society was there, the state gave the house to the city. I've met people who said that the state was divesting itself of property at the time [the 1970s]. It sounds crazy, but they were.

LC: I'm wondering if that was the time when Ronald Reagan was the governor. Because maybe he was trying to trim [the] government.

CR: Good point. It might have been. It was 1971. That's when the house became a city cultural historic landmark. My other theory about why the state might have given it away [was that] the San Fernando Earthquake [happened] in January 1971 [it actually happened in February 1971], and in the middle of 1971, the state gave the house to the city. The main house has never had any significant earthquake damage, but the casitas out back did. One of them had a second level that collapsed in that earthquake. My theory is that the state was like "Here, city! *You* have the unreinforced masonry building!" But the city *was* running it, so it made sense that it belonged to the city. During that whole time [since 1965], the Historical Society of Southern California [HSSC] was there. They had an operating agreement with the city. What ended up happening was that the historical society was trying to raise money . . . to do repairs to the house, so they began negotiating [again] with the city, and they couldn't come to terms on it. So the HSSC left after fifty years. The last day I opened [the] house for the HSSC was February 1, 2015.

LC: Then you were able to segue into becoming an employee of the city?

CR: Correct. What ended up happening was they wanted to keep the house open. [The] Department of Recreation and Parks took over, and they needed a park employee there to open the house. I volunteered because I was so freaked out that they were going to close the house. I reached out and said, "I'll come in for *free*, at least until something gets sorted out." Of course, I had nothing to do with the negotiations, so I was kind of neutral to them. They said, "We need somebody who can keep the place open and answer questions. Let's just hire the guy who's already here."

LC: I suppose it helped your image when KCET did their thing [*Charles Lummis: Reimagining the American West*], and you were a prominent person in the documentary.

CR: It kind of helped among Rec. and Parks people, yeah. Rec. and Parks directly manages a couple of small museums, but most of the museums that are under [their] purview operate the way the HSSC did—where there's another nonprofit there, and they kind of do their own thing.

LC: Like the Gamble House?

CR: Well, that's in the city of Pasadena. Every historic site in LA is different. If you go to the Parks and Rec. website, you can see all the historic sites that they own [there are eleven of them], but they don't necessarily operate [them]. They only operate three, including the Charles Lummis House.

LC: What are the other two?

CR: The Banning House—

LC: In Wilmington?

CR: At the Banning House, they have a very active friends group [Friends of Banning Museum]. They have a kids' store, they collect donations, they do repairs. They have a very passionate, very active friends group. [At first] I assumed they were [independent], but I found out that the director of the Banning Museum and [a] couple of the staff [members] are Rec. and Parks employees.

LC: And the third one?

CR: The Point Fermin Lighthouse in San Pedro.

LC: That's interesting.

CR: There are a couple [of] historic sites that are owned by the city that are under the purview of the DCA [Department of Cultural Affairs]. I think the reason for that is they were places that were given to the city specifically to be art centers or art spaces.

LC: One of them is probably the Barnsdall House?

CR: Correct. Aline Barnsdall gave the Hollyhock House to the city to be an arts center. They have an art gallery there, but the house is a historic [structure, designed by Frank Lloyd Wright], and the DCA manages that. The other places . . . there's the Warner Grand Theatre in San Pedro, which is a historic theater.

LC: Is it connected to the Warner Brothers?

CR: Yeah, it was a Warner Theater from when movie studios still had their own theaters. Then there's the Watts Towers. It's [a] historic site, but it's an art center. And the McGroarty Arts Center.

LC: Over in Sunland?

CR: Yeah, which is a craftsman kind of house, but now it's an art center. But all the other historic sites in the city are under the purview of the Department of Rec. and Parks. What the city of Los Angeles is lacking is a department whose area is to manage or at least work with the nonprofits that manage these historic sites. We have a very recreation-focused parks department in Los Angeles, and so part of the issue with historic sites that are owned by the city [is that] you have a department that doesn't really understand what you do in a historic house museum. In the city of LA, we have a Department of *Recreation* and Parks.

LC: I see *recreation* first.

CR: I feel like there really should be a department, or at least a division within Rec. and Parks, whose purview it is to deal with these historic resources that the city owns.

LC: If someone [has] never heard of Charles Lummis before, what are some important things about him worth mentioning?

CR: He was so accomplished; he did all these things. He was a writer, an editor, a librarian, an architectural preservationist.

LC: One of the first reporters for the *LA Times*?

CR: A local reporter, yes. He was a city editor. He was a Native American advocate.

LC: He founded the first museum [in Los Angeles].

CR: Right. The first museum, and all his writings, and editing the magazine . . . most of what he did, what his legacy is as a big promoter of the history and cultures of the southwest. There were other people doing that, too, but what Lummis did was emphasize the history of the southwest—the history of Spanish colonial settlement and Native American cultures as something that we should embrace as part of the history of the United States. So, in his own special way, he was thinking of an alternative perspective on the history of the United States. You see that in his editorials. He was like "Oh, we have this rich history here." His way of embracing the history of the southwest is almost him rejecting his New England roots. There's a really good comprehensive biography about Lummis.

LC: I got that one.

CR: Right. *American Character* by a guy named Mark Thompson.[4] That book is really well written, really well researched. Everything I know about Lummis is from that source. You get Lummis's life, and he doesn't just venerate him; it's objective.

LC: I think in today's #MeToo culture, it seems the womanizing aspect is—

CR: That's the worst! That's the worst part. Even in the context of his times, it's like Lummis was a letch. But I'm more interested in what Lummis was trying to do and how that legacy is still pertinent today. He's a good vehicle for getting people [to start] thinking about the history of the southwest as important and as a part of the history of the United States. It's difficult to get from point A to point B [when talking with visitors to the Lummis House]. Usually, we only get halfway, or it's just all Lummis because there's enough there, and people are interested. But every once in a while, I can get to the bigger point

---

4   Mark Thompson, *American Character: The Curious Life of Charles Fletcher Lummis* (New York: Arcade, 2001).

[his legacy in terms of the southwest], and that's when I feel most satisfied about my job there. Lummis had a very broad idea of the southwest, and he tied it very much to the history of Mexico and [to] the history of the indigenous peoples, not [only] in the southwestern United States but [also] in Mexico and Central and South America. He tied it all together; he had this very broad idea of what the history of the southwestern United States was. To that end, Lummis wrote a book about the history of Mexico. We have a copy of it on display. A young Latino came in, and he saw a book [by Lummis] that was written in Spanish about the history of Mexico. I was like "Yeah, remember this was Mexico!" So he was thinking the history of Mexico includes California. I said that to him, and you could see in his face a sense of "my history . . . I'm in a place that reflects my history, too. I'm not an outsider!" Moments like that are the most satisfying.

LC: Yeah, the majority of my students are Latino, and sometimes it's like a revelation to them [that] the names of all our biggest cities—San Francisco, Sacramento, San Diego, Los Angeles— are all Spanish terms.

CR: The fact that these very old cities are created on an axis, like downtown Los Angeles or Santa Barbara or even Santa Ana— if you look at older cities in California, their downtown areas are a grid on an axis. That's because there was a mandate by the king of Spain.

LC: There had to be a plaza and [a] church.

CR: The street grids had to be on an angle for some reason. But that's tied to Spanish colonization. When California became a part of the United States, there was a harsh divide. Fresno is the best example. Look at a map of Fresno. The downtown area's on an angle, and then when it became a part of the United States, they did a grid on a north/south axis.

LC: I didn't know that.

CR: Yeah, the city of Los Angeles, downtown, is on an angle, and San Fernando, Santa Ana, Santa Barbara, Old Town San Diego, and new downtown San Diego are on the American north/south grid. But that's kind of a tangent. What I'm more interested in is what Lummis was trying to do in his own way. Lummis himself sort of reinvented himself as this ultimate southwesterner. He accomplished a lot of great things in his life, but he also had this massive ego. Sometimes I wonder how much of the Lummis [mystique] came from Lummis himself. He sort of invented his own importance as a historic figure.

LC: Yeah, I still have the impression that in the "tramp across the continent" [Lummis's walk from Cincinnati, Ohio, to Los Angeles, from 1884 to 1885], he probably got a few rides.

CR: I think that's very much confirmed. People have analyzed the timeline, and there are a couple [of] spots that don't make sense. And specific things that happened to him, even when I was reading it, I'm like, "This is really stretching the realms of believability!"

LC: Like breaking his arm and setting it himself!

CR: That was the one that did it for me. I'm like, "I'm sorry, I can't [believe this!]." But Lummis sort of encapsulates LA.

LC: He reinvents himself.

CR: He reinvents himself as this ultimate southwesterner. It's his own creation; it's very artificial.

LC: Some analysts have said that. What's our biggest culture in LA? Movies, entertainment . . . it's all artificial.

CR: But he was before the movies. So it almost makes you ask: Is there something just inherent about California that makes people . . . I guess it's just the whole idea of the West: I can come out to the West, I can come out to this new uncharted territory and reinvent a new person.

LC: Yeah. That's the story of Hollywood. New Jersey was actually the original center of the old nickelodeons, but [Thomas] Edison controlled everything. When somebody tried to make a movie, they found themselves being sued by him, so they ended up coming out here.

CR: Yeah, it's the Wild West.

LC: So 1907 and 1908—that's why they came to Hollywood. And if things went really badly, they could pack up all their stuff and go into Mexico. That really was what started Hollywood, the idea of escaping the rules.

CR: But it's the idea of reinvention: I'm coming out to this place where nobody knows me, and I can kind of decide that this is going to be my image now.

14

A PARTIAL HISTORY OF LOS ANGELES

Los Angeles is a city of juxtapositions, where the old and the new collide to create something uniquely beautiful.

—Rachel Bilson

AFTER ALMOST FIFTEEN years of teaching professional development classes for teachers and visiting all kinds of sites important in the development of Los Angeles, I've become something of a local history nerd. After I began driving for Lyft, that background experience came in handy when I was talking with passengers about interesting places to visit around LA. It really makes a difference when a local happens to know a lot about local history. So here is a brief, partial history of the town where I have lived for most of my fiftysomething years. When I say a *partial* history, I mean that in two senses of the term. It's a partial history because it does not tell the whole story; it focuses only on the parts that I have learned about and consider important enough to include here. Any real historian who reads it is likely to say, "Hey, he didn't say anything about old so-and-so" or "Why didn't he mention the blah blah blah?" But that brings us to the other meaning of the term *partial*. When someone reports only facts, their writing is said to be impartial. Because I know this is a mixture of facts and opinions, I willingly admit that it is a *partial* history in both senses of the term. I am telling the stories that I find interesting and integral to the history of Los Angeles.

And that history is amazing. Forty-four people arrived to start a little town chartered by King Charles III of Spain in the same year (1781) that George Washington accepted the surrender of General Cornwallis on the other side of North America and the American Revolution came to an end (at least, the fighting stopped, even though the treaty to end the war wasn't signed until two years later, in 1783). The forty-four people who arrived in 1781 to start a new little town were of Spanish, Native American, and African ancestry. So Los Angeles was already a multiethnic place from the moment it began. The little town gradually grew, as more Californios arrived in the Spanish territory of California in the early 1800s.

One of these Californio families first became established in Southern California in 1784, just a few years after the founding of El Pueblo de la Reyna de Los Angeles. The first Spanish land grant in California went to Juan José Dominguez, a retired soldier who came to California with the Portolá expedition (the first recorded exploration of California's interior by Europeans from 1769 to 1770) and later accompanied Father (now Saint) Junípero Serra. The same Spanish king who approved the founding of Los Angeles (Carlos III) also approved a rather generous land grant of seventy-five thousand acres to the retired soldier. There wasn't much on it at the time, but the land stretches from present-day Los Angeles Harbor across the area that's now called the South Bay and includes the land occupied by the communities of San Pedro, Rancho Palos Verdes, Torrance,

Redondo Beach, Hermosa Beach, Manhattan Beach, Lawndale, Hawthorne, Carson, Compton, and—you guessed it—Dominguez Hills. The old soldier died in 1809 without any children, so the land passed to his nephew, Cristobal Dominguez. Cristobal allowed a young man named José Dolores Sepulveda to run cattle on the part of his land that was now Rancho Palos Verdes. Later, a dispute took place, and Dominguez told Sepulveda to leave. He refused, which turned into a long-running legal battle that eventually resulted in the Sepulveda family's ownership of Rancho Palos Verdes and the name of the longest street in LA, Sepulveda Boulevard.

*José Dolores Sepulveda
(1793–1824), the young man
whose dispute with the Dominguez
family shaped local history.*

*Manuel Dominguez
(1803–1882), one of the key players"
in the story of LA, especially the South
Bay and surrounding areas.*

José Dolores Sepulveda was the son of a Spanish soldier named Juan José Sepulveda and his wife, Maria Candelaria de Redondo. His mother's name lives on in the city of Redondo Beach. José's dispute with the Dominguez family eventually resulted in a significant acquisition of land for the Sepulveda clan. Unfortunately for him, however, he met an untimely death at the age of thirty when he was traveling with four companions and stopped at La Purisima Mission (near the present-day town of Lompoc) on the afternoon of February 21, 1824. As he and his companions stopped to arrange for the night's lodging, they were unaware that the Chumash Indians were in revolt. They were ambushed at the mission and killed by the Chumash. However, his family continued the long-running legal dispute for the land that would become Palos Verdes.

The Dominguez family did not win the dispute with the Sepulvedas, but Manuel Dominguez (Cristobal's son) lived a long and influential life. By the time he died in 1882, he had influenced, via his collaboration with Phineas Banning, the development of the Harbor of Los Angeles and the stagecoach lines that later became the rail lines and then the Harbor (110) Freeway. He guided William Mulholland into the kind of work that would lead to his role as the water czar of Los Angeles; successfully married his daughters to men named Carson, Del Amo, and Watson (names that live on today in the California city of Carson, Carson Street, the Del Amo Mall in Torrance, Del Amo Boulevard, and the Watson Land Company); and started a legacy that would lead to the development of the aerospace industry in Southern California. When Manuel's son-in-law hosted the first major airshow in America in 1910 at the Dominguez Rancho (in present-day Carson), it was attended by a few young men whose names would become synonymous with the development of aerospace: William Boeing, Donald Wills Douglas (which later become part of McDonnell Douglas in 1967), and Glenn Curtiss (whose company would manufacture many of the airplanes flown in World War I and is now part of the Curtiss-Wright Corporation). But we'll come back to this later.

In 1821, Mexico got its independence from Spain, and El Pueblo de la Reyna de Los Angeles grew in the style of towns in areas originally colonized by Spain: with a main plaza, a church, and a few shops. In 1845, the last Mexican governor of California, Pío Pico, made El Pueblo (Los Angeles) the capital of California and built the fancy hotel that stands to this day next to the Plaza Olvera and Olvera Street. Soon after, the Mexican-American War broke out, and Pío Pico fled to Mexico. In 1847, Pío's brother, Andrés Pico, led Californio troops in a few pitched battles against American troops. The Californios actually killed more American troops than vice versa, but Pico realized that much larger American armies were headed his way, and he surrendered on behalf of his vastly outnumbered Californio troops to American forces under John Frémont at the Campo de Cahuenga. This historic site still stands, across the street from Universal Studios. The Pico brothers' name lives on in the cities of Pico Rivera, Pico Union and Pico Boulevard.

Pío Pico, the last Mexican governor of California.

Andrés Pico, who commanded the last Mexican/Californio troops to engage American forces in battle.

California became part of the United States (along with territories that would become the southwestern states) in 1848. The gold rush of 1849 brought large numbers of people to California, but most of them settled in the northern part of the state. Los Angeles was still a small town of 1,610, according to the census of 1850, the first year it was recorded. The census of 1860 noted the population at 4,385—four times the number from ten years previously but still not a big city. The Civil War began in 1861, which probably explains why the population grew by only about one thousand by the census of 1870. In the 1870s, the railroads started reaching Los Angeles, and that's a good reason why the population almost doubled by the census of 1880, which recorded the number of residents as 11,183. One hundred years after its founding, LA became a city of just over eleven thousand souls, but there was still no clear sign that it would become the second largest city in the US in about the next fifty to sixty years.

Phineas Banning, who was responsible for the building of the Port of Los Angeles as well as the founding of the city of Wilmington.

Collis Huntington, who brought the railroads to Los Angeles (and other cities of the Southwest).

However, several remarkable things happened in the next few decades due to a few amazing and industrious individuals. Phineas Banning was one of them. Because of his vision and tenacity, the Port of Los Angeles was built and quickly put LA on a par with sea-trading cities throughout the world that were centuries older. In the 1800s, most commerce between countries was still being done by ships. On land, most things moved by stagecoach and, increasingly, railroads. The stage line that Banning established between the Port of Los Angeles (present-day San Pedro) and the city center set the stage for rail lines and eventually for the Harbor Freeway. The city of Wilmington was named by Banning himself, in honor of his hometown of Wilmington, Delaware. Banning High School, as well as the city of Banning, were named in his honor. Meanwhile, Collis Huntington and his business partners built rail lines into Los Angeles, first from San Francisco and later from the other states of the union, and the number of people visiting and/or moving to Los Angeles continued to increase. The population of Los Angeles quadrupled from 11,183 in 1880 to more than 50,000 in 1890. The city of Huntington Beach and the Huntington Library and Museum are two popular tourist destinations named after Huntington.

In the later 1800s, two other large-scale land developers and visionaries whose names became fixtures of local LA lore were Elias J. "Lucky" Baldwin and Abbot Kinney. Baldwin's nickname was Lucky because he seemed to have incredible luck in both gambling and business. Baldwin decided to purchase, develop, and build significant places around Southern California. The Santa Anita Racetrack and the Los Angeles Arboretum were his children, and the city of Baldwin Park, the Baldwin Hills neighborhood, and several other places with Baldwin in their titles are named for him. Abbot Kinney was a visionary whose visit to Venice, Italy, led to the construction of the canals and waterways of Venice, California. Most of them would be closed in the 1920s due to health concerns, but a few survive to this day.

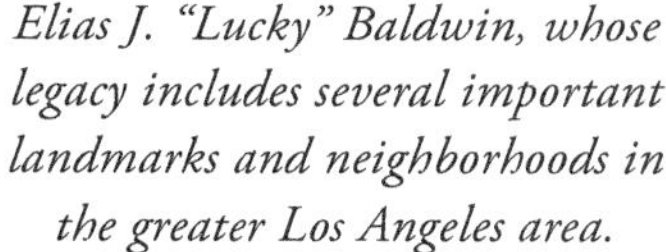

Elias J. "Lucky" Baldwin, whose legacy includes several important landmarks and neighborhoods in the greater Los Angeles area.

Abbot Kinney, whose visit to Venice, Italy, led to the creation of Venice, California.

Meanwhile, back at the rancho (Rancho Dominguez Hills), Manuel Dominguez makes a deal with Phineas Banning to the effect that the stage lines, and later the railroad lines between downtown LA and San Pedro Harbor, which had to pass through Dominguez's land, would include a stop at the rancho. In 1877, a penniless William Mulholland arrived in LA but was unable to find work. He headed for the Port of Los Angeles and found a ship bound for somewhere else. He had to stop at Dominguez Rancho on the way there, never making it to the harbor because he was offered a job by the aging Manuel Dominguez, digging wells on the rancho. In 1880, he was hired as a ditch digger by the newly formed Los Angeles Water Company and worked his way up the ladder, eventually becoming one of the most important players in the growth of LA.

Edward Doheny,
the prospector who first discovered
oil in Los Angeles and who went
from rags to riches and
started the oil boom.

William Mulholland,
the man who brought water
to the sprawling city of
Los Angeles.

Then oil was discovered by Edward Doheny, which started the Southern California oil boom of the 1890s. It may seem strange to us today, but in the early 1900s, Los Angeles was the biggest oil producer in the country. Doheny would also start the oil company that is now called Pemex, the national (government-run) oil company of Mexico. The population doubled to 102,479 by 1900 and then tripled to more than 300,000 by 1910. Hollywood merged with Los Angeles around that time, and the film industry arrived en masse, as filmmakers flocked to a locale where they could easily bring a film crew to a beach with an ocean, mountains, desert, or forest within a few hours. Los Angeles quickly became the entertainment capital of the world, a distinction it retains to this day.

In the early 1900s, this question arose: How will the necessary water be supplied to support the booming population? Most big cities are built next to a large flowing river, something Los Angeles never had, and the amount of rainfall is never enough to support a large population. The question was answered through the energy, passion, and vision of the formerly penniless Irish immigrant William Mulholland. He worked his way up the Los Angeles City Water Company, studying books on science and engineering in the evenings, after days of physical labor. Later, he read works of great literature, became a naturalized American citizen in 1886, and was named the chief engineer of the Los Angeles Water Department in 1902. Mulholland solved the problem of how to bring water to Los Angeles by supervising and carrying out the construction of the Los Angeles Aqueduct, a massive 237-mile-long project that employed five thousand workers and eventually brought water from the Owens Valley to Southern California.

Mulholland's career came to a crashing end (quite literally) with the disastrous collapse of the Saint Francis Dam in 1928, which claimed an estimated six hundred lives and has been described as the worst civil engineering disaster of the twentieth century. At the Los Angeles coroner's inquest, Mulholland stated, "Don't blame anyone else. Just fasten it on me. If there was an error in human judgment, I was the human." Other than Mulholland Drive, if William Mulholland is remembered at all by current residents of LA, it's generally for the Saint Francis Dam disaster, and that's a pity, because everyone who lives in Los Angeles to this day continues to benefit from the waterworks he put in place, some of which are still in use just under the city sidewalks and streets where we live and move and conduct our business.

Throughout the 1920s and 1930s, the film industry continued to grow and helped to insulate Los Angeles from the effects of the Great Depression, which caused great suffering throughout the rest of the country. Hollywood became a mecca where the beautiful people made movies and partied in a sort of opulent dream while the rest of the country was in desperate need of the kind of escapism provided by movies. Filmmakers like Cecille B. DeMille created lavish productions, and the stars of the silver screen captivated audiences around the world. Stars such as Rudolph Valentino, Claudette Colbert, Marlene Dietrich, Errol Flynn, Clark Gable, and, later, Humphrey Bogart and Lauren Bacall captured the attention and the imagination of audiences everywhere, as movie theaters sprung up across the country and eventually the world.

The movie industry's roots started back East with Thomas Edison's invention of the kinetoscope in the 1890s. However, the center of gravity for movie production became California around 1908 when filmmakers relocated to present-day Hollywood to escape prosecution by Edison's lawyers for copyright infringement. Similarly, the origin of motorized flight happened near Kitty Hawk, North Carolina, with the Wright Brothers in 1903. But the center of the aerospace industry became Southern California within the next two decades after the Los Angeles International Air Meet at Dominguez Field in 1910, which the Wright Brothers refused to attend. But several people did attend who are now household names in the history and present production of aircraft: William Boeing, Donald Wills Douglas, Glenn Curtiss, and others.

Southern California quickly became front and center for aviation production as a result of the efforts of Harry Chandler, publisher of the *Los Angeles Times*, who used his influence to convince aviation companies to come to the area. Other powerful people of the time contributed to the trend, such as Harry Culver, the founder of Culver City, who played a huge role in establishing LAX at its current location in the late 1920s. The following extract (from the website of the Hughes Industrial Historic District) describes the growth of the aerospace industry in Southern California during and a few years before the twenties and thirties:

> Consequently, Los Angeles quickly became home to several of the world's largest aviation firms. In 1916, the Lockheed Brothers migrated from Northern to Southern California and set up a small aircraft production firm.

Within a few years, they became major suppliers to the British Royal Air Force, and by the end of World War II, they had over 60,000 employees. In 1920, Harry Chandler persuaded Donald Douglas to open a company in the region. His firm Douglas Aircraft first rented facilities in an abandoned movie studio in Santa Monica and went on to become one of the chief manufacturers of aircraft in the United States. Jack Northrop opened his first airplane company in Los Angeles in the 1920s, but soon after, merged it with other firms. He started another company in 1939, which benefitted enormously from the impending Second World War, and became yet another aircraft giant. Howard Hughes' Hughes Aircraft Company, founded in 1932, started in a rented hangar in Burbank, but ultimately grew to encompass 1,300 acres at the edge of Culver City and became one of the largest industrial employers in the state. The move of North American Aviation, later Rockwell International, to Inglewood in 1935 solidified the region as a center of aircraft production.

Howard Hughes (a.k.a. the aviator), who was deeply involved in the film and aerospace industries of Los Angeles from the 1930s to the 1970s.

During World War II, Los Angeles became a center of production of ships and airplanes for the war effort. After the war, the aerospace industry continued to grow, mainly due to the big demand for airplanes, as air travel for passengers became the long-distance travel mode of choice, and to the Cold War, which fueled military growth and its demand for up-to-date aircraft.

In the census of 1930, the population of Los Angeles topped the one million mark; it reached about four million by 2016. In the 1930s, the dream factory continued to grow and attract people from all around the United States. There were also large numbers of migrants to California who had lost their farms and homes in the Great Depression, as described in John Steinbeck's powerful novel *The Grapes of Wrath*. The trend of people coming to Los Angeles continued throughout the coming decades. Large numbers of Latinos, Filipinos, Arabs, Armenians, Southeast Asians (after the wars in Korea and Vietnam), and Europeans continued to arrive in Los Angeles, making it the second largest concentration of the population in the US.

The little settlement that started in 1781 had become the improbable global metropolis that exploded into a world-class city in a few generations. As the United States had come to symbolize a place where anyone could come from the Old World and re-create themselves from an impoverished peasant into a successful citizen (the American dream), Los Angeles grew up to symbolize the newest world of the New World: a place where average people could come to re-create themselves into new people. Many came for economic opportunity, as the oil industry, then the automobile, aerospace, and film industries all grew exponentially throughout the twentieth century. Doheny grew rich through his discovery of oil. J. Paul Getty also became rich through the oil industry and started the oil companies of the Middle East. Then oil production gradually receded in importance in Southern California, as the movie, aerospace, and automobile industries become prominent. In time, the aerospace and auto industries became bigger in other states, but the one industry over which Los Angeles retains unquestionable dominance is entertainment. Hollywood is still Hollywood, even in the 2020s, and nowhere else on earth surpasses it for film production . . . well, at least not yet.

There is much to admire about LA. For all its faults, it's a place of great beauty and fascinating history, and it's an exciting mix of cultures, people, and things to see and do. Like any big city, it has its share of problems: not only broken dreams but also crime, violence, and vice. But it also has some interesting stories and amazing people. Sometimes as I drive along the Pacific Coast Highway and notice the sun setting over the ocean, or somewhere in Hollywood and notice the golden sunlight bathing the beautiful Hollywood Hills, or the breathtaking view of the city at night from various points of the winding curves of Mulholland Drive, it seems like this is still the coolest place to live and drive.

15

ONE FOR THE WOMEN OF LA HISTORY

It was clear that long-term settlement of these lands could not be achieved by men alone. It was only when women could be persuaded to go west alongside their men that the business of putting down permanent roots could begin. Homesteads and farms would then be built, the land would be plowed and crops sown, animals bred and husbanded. Most importantly, future generations would be born to carry on the work their parents had begun.

—Katie Hickman,
Brave Hearted: The Women of the American West

AFTER COMPLETING THE previous chapter, I realized that it focused on several important men in the history of LA. But there were important women in that story, too, and so this chapter describes some of them.

Women were part of the story of LA from the day of its founding. When the first eleven families arrived to start El Pueblo de la Reyna de Los Angeles in September 1781, eleven were wives of eleven male settlers, and ten were daughters of the married couples. Five of the married women were described as mulatta (mixed Spanish and African ancestry) and six were described as Indian (Native American or Indigenous). By contrast, two of their husbands were Spanish (one born in Spain, and one born in Mexico), two were Black (African), two were mulatto, one was mestizo (mixed Spanish and Indian), and four were Indian (Native American). From the very beginning of Los Angeles, there was a mixture of races and cultures.

One of the most noteworthy examples was the granddaughter of one of the original founding couples, José Moreno and Maria Guadalupe Gertrudis Perez. Maria lived for almost one hundred years, until 1860. She was the last surviving original settler of Los Angeles. Her granddaughter, Catalina Carmen Moreno, became the wife of Don Andrés Pico, the military commander of the Californios who fought American troops during the Mexican-American War. He would later sign the Articles of Capitulation with Lt. Col. John C. Frémont that ended the fighting in California in 1847.

Another woman played a more important role in the signing of that treaty. Her name was Bernarda Ruiz de Rodríguez. She was born in the mission town of Santa Barbara in 1802. Bernarda married at the age of fifteen and

Doña Bernarda Ruiz de Rodriguez, as she might have appeared when she met with John Frémont on Christmas Eve, 1846.

was widowed as a young mother of four sons. She and her children operated an express mail service between Santa Barbara and Mexico City. When the Mexican-American War started in 1846, her sons joined the Californio (Mexican) army. Then Lt. Col. John C. Frémont arrived in Santa Barbara with some four hundred American troops. Bernarda feared for her sons' lives, dreading the possibility that they would have to fight against Frémont's troops.

She requested a ten-minute audience with Frémont. He granted the request, and they met on Christmas Eve, 1846. The ten minutes turned into several hours, as she laid out plans for a "generous peace" that would end the fighting in California, release prisoners on both sides, and allow Mexican citizens to return to Mexico, if they so chose. Frémont would later describe the meeting with Bernarda in his memoirs: "She wished me to take into my mind this plan of settlement, to which she would influence her people . . . Naturally her character and sound reasoning had its influence with me."[5]

After meeting with Frémont, Bernarda sought out and spoke with Andrés Pico. He and Frémont would meet at the Campo de Cahuenga and sign the Treaty of Cahuenga on January 13, 1847, which ended the fighting between American and Californio troops in California. The war would not end until the following year (1848), after American troops invaded and captured Mexico City. But the Treaty of Guadalupe Hidalgo, which ended the Mexican-American War, was deeply influenced by the Treaty of Cahuenga, which was based on the proposals offered to Lt. Col. Frémont on that fateful Christmas Eve in Santa Barbara by Bernarda Ruiz de Rodríguez.

During the same decade in which Bernarda became a young widow (the 1820s), Manuel Dominguez was building the Dominguez Rancho Adobe, which still stands to this day. He did not have any surviving male children, but he managed to hold on to his family's

---

5 Cecilia Rasmussen, "Woman Helped Bring a Peaceful End to Mexican-American War," *Los Angeles Times*, May 5, 2002, www.latimes.com/archives/la-xpm-2002-may-05-me-then5-story.html.

ancestral land by passing it on to his daughters, two of whom married men whose last names would become prominent to local geography: Maria Victoria Dominguez would marry George Henry Carson, and the city of Carson, California, would derive its name from their family. Susana Delfina Dominguez would marry a prominent Spaniard named Dr. Gregorio del Amo, and his name would be the basis for a prominent South Bay thoroughfare, Del Amo Boulevard, and for the gigantic Del Amo Fashion Center in Torrance.

Another woman whose common-law marriage would play a great part in local LA history was Maria del Espiritu Chijulla Leonis. Miguel Leonis was a Basque immigrant who came to Los Angeles in 1854. Five years later, he was the ranch foreman at Rancho El Escorpión, which was a land concession made to three Chumash Indians of Mission San Fernando. He was also united in common-law marriage with the daughter of one of the Chumash chieftains, Maria del Espiritu. Eventually, he would make various real estate deals that would result in his ownership of a large part of the western San Fernando Valley by the 1880s. After building a massive real estate empire (big enough that he was once described as the King of Calabasas), Miguel died as a result of injuries sustained from a fast-moving wagon accident in 1889. In his will, he left the vast majority of his amassed fortune to his Basque relatives in France, with only a comparatively modest sum to Espiritu. She hired an attorney to challenge the pronouncement, and a sixteen-year legal battle ensued. Historian Dinna Rivera-Pitt describes the significance of Espiritu's legal victory when the court finally decided that she was the rightful heir of the lands of Miguel Leonis: "As a

Spanish-speaking Chumash Indian woman, her legal victory was an extraordinary achievement for the time. After receiving news of her legal triumph, a photo of Espiritu sitting in her lawyer's Calabasas office was taken for the local newspapers."

Once, while I was on a walking tour of downtown Los Angeles (organized by the Los Angeles Conservancy), I learned about an amazing woman named Bridget "Biddy" Mason. Her story symbolizes the California dream at its best—how a person can come to California and re-create themselves, work hard, pursue a dream, and achieve tremendous success. Bridget was born and raised in slavery and brought to California as a slave in 1851, along with members of her family who were also slaves. One of her daughters became romantically involved with a young man who decided to tell the LA County sheriff that slaves were being illegally held, since slavery was not legal in California. The sheriff gathered a posse and appre-

Bridget "Biddy" Mason was born a slave in 1818, but she achieved her freedom in California and became one of the first prominent citizens and landowners of Los Angeles until her death in 1891.

hended the owner of Bridget and her family. Later, she petitioned LA District Judge Benjamin Hayes for her freedom, and she won her case. She moved with her family to Los Angeles and worked as a midwife and nurse, saving her money. Eventually, she purchased land in what is now downtown LA. In time, she organized the First AME (African Methodist Episcopal) Church, which is the oldest predominantly Black church in LA. She also founded an elementary school for Black children and a traveler's aid center and donated to numerous charities, fed and sheltered poor and homeless people, and visited prisons. This amazing woman probably never had much formal education, but she still made her mark on the development of Los Angeles through hard work, an unshakable faith in God, and a commitment to helping others.

Another female transplant who came to Southern California in the late nineteenth century and who had a tremendous influence on the development of local culture was Helen Hunt Jackson. She was born in Amherst, Massachusetts, on October 15, 1830. She lost both parents while still in her teens, but her father provided for her education before he died. Helen was educated in New York, where she was a classmate and lifelong friend of the poet Emily Dickinson. As a young woman, she endured tremendous suffering, as both of her children died from diseases while they were still very young, and her husband was killed in an accident in 1863. She wrote poetry that reflected her sorrows, and it was published in literary magazines such as the *Atlantic* and the *Independent*; it also caught the attention of Ralph Waldo Emerson, who started using some of her poems in his public readings.

In 1879, Jackson attended a lecture by Chief Standing Bear about the creation of the Great Sioux Reservation in 1868. Angered by the injustices described by the Indian chief, she wrote a book titled *A Century of Dishonor*. After it was published in 1881, she sent a copy to every member of Congress, with this quote from Benjamin Franklin printed on the cover: "Look upon your hands: they are stained with the blood of your relations." After making several enemies in Washington, DC, Jackson decided to move to California to have some respite. However, once she learned about the suffering of the Mission Indians—members of the Chumash and Tongva (and other) tribes who, after the dissolution of the missions and the annexation of California by the United States were suffering tremendously by American rule—she went into action again.

She sought and obtained the help of the US Indian agent Abbot Kinney (the same man who founded Venice Beach, as described in the previous chapter) and traveled throughout Southern California, documenting the maltreatment of the Indians. In 1883, she completed her report and appealed to Congress to take action to help the Indians. A bill based on her recommendations passed in the Senate but died in the House of Representatives. Frustrated but undeterred, she decided to write a novel that would "set forth some Indian experiences in a way to move people's hearts." Just as the book *Uncle Tom's Cabin*, which was written by her friend Harriet Beecher Stowe, had raised public awareness of the evil of slavery before the Civil War, Jackson hoped to write a novel that would raise public awareness of the maltreatment of the Indians in California under American governance. "If I could write a story," she wrote, "that would do for the Indian one-hundredth part what *Uncle Tom's Cabin* did for the Negro, I would be thankful the rest of my life." In 1884, her novel *Ramona* was published. It achieved widespread success and has never been out of print since that time. A writer for the *North American Review* described *Ramona* as "unquestionably the best novel yet produced by an American woman" and named it as one of the two most ethical novels of the nineteenth century (the other being *Uncle Tom's Cabin*). *Ramona* has been adapted several times in film, radio broadcast, and television, with the most recent being a Mexican telenovela of the same name in the year 2000. The Ramona Pageant is an annual outdoor play that has been performed every year since 1923 in Hemet, California.

Helen Hunt Jackson, as she may have appeared at the time of the publication of her novel Ramona in 1884.

An artist's depiction of the star-crossed lovers in Jackson's novel Ramona.

If we are discussing women who contributed to the cultural heritage of Los Angeles, we can't pass over Arabella Huntington. She was the second wife of Collis Huntington (the wealthy railway tycoon and industrialist described in the previous chapter). She had been the caretaker of his ailing first wife, and after she passed away in 1884, Collis married Arabella later that same year. Collis passed away in 1900, and in 1913, she married Collis's nephew, Henry Huntington. He was the founder of the Huntington Library, Museum, and Gardens in San Marino. But it was Arabella who was the force behind the amazing collection of art and manuscripts that reside there now. These include a Gutenberg Bible (the first book made with the Gutenberg printing press); a medieval vellum manuscript of Chaucer's *Canterbury Tales*; a first edition Shakespeare folio (printed in the first year Shakespeare's plays were published, 1621); original editions of poetry by John Milton, William Wordsworth, and Samuel Taylor Coleridge; and letters by Mark Twain, Abraham Lincoln, and various other well-known writers, scientists, and social and political thinkers. With all its primary sources, the Huntington has become a center for scholars conducting research and publishing articles and books in various areas of study. All of this is there because of Arabella Huntington's vision and interest in education and culture. She may not have earned the massive fortune that made the Huntington possible, but she knew how to spend it in a way that would enrich the greater Los Angeles area for generations to come.

A portrait of Arabella Huntington as a young woman in 1870, probably a few years before she first met Collis Huntington.

This picture of Arabella Huntington was taken in 1915, two years after her marriage to Henry.

Like Arabella Huntington, May Rindge, the Queen of Malibu, became important because of her connection to her husband, but she also achieved a great deal after his death in 1905. The full story of this power couple is described in *The King and Queen of Malibu: The True Story of the Battle for Paradise* by David K. Randall. After they had three children, they purchased their Malibu land and pursued the dream of living on a secluded rancho by the sea. After the untimely death of her husband, Frederick, at the age of forty-seven, she became the sole owner of the family estate and spent years fighting developers, railroad companies, the federal government, and the state of California in an effort to preserve the beauty of her Malibu property. Eventually, she lost, and so the throughfare now known as the Pacific Coast Highway was built. Perhaps she decided that if you can't beat them, join them, because she eventually decided to start the Malibu Movie Colony and built, rented, and later sold cottages to early Hollywood stars such as Bing Crosby and Mary Pickford. The Malibu Colony still exists today and continues to host some of the biggest celebrities in film, TV, and sports.

The last woman of LA history to be described is arguably the most important. She was born Chastina Rix in Oakland, California, in 1881. She changed her name to Christine as a teenager, studied art and design at Mills College in Oakland, and then married briefly. After her first marriage failed, she wed an attorney named Jerome Hough, with whom she had two children. They moved to Los Angeles because of his film industry work around 1920. Not long after that, Hough died from a stroke, leaving Christine a struggling widow with two small children and no reliable source of income. How did she support herself in the early 1920s? That question will need to remain un-

This portrait of Christine Sterling was taken in the 1920s, the decade in which she began her campaign to preserve Olvera Street and the Avila Adobe.

answered for now, since the details about her life are sparse and difficult to find. But what is clear is that by the latter 1920s, she had found a new purpose and a new name.

She first visited the old plaza area of Los Angeles in 1926. She wrote in her journal that although it was the "birthplace of the city," it was "forsaken and forgotten." She continued: "Down a dirty alley,

I discovered an old adobe, dignified even in its decay." The building she saw, the Avila Adobe, still stands today because of her work and is currently the oldest house in Los Angeles (it was constructed in 1818). Sterling stood in the abandoned alley and stared out at twenty-six buildings that were scheduled for demolition. She was struck by a vision: "I closed my eyes and thought of the plaza as a Spanish-American social and commercial center. It would furnish Los Angeles with the greatest tourist attraction she may ever have—a spot of beauty as a gesture of appreciation for our historical past."

This picture was taken in January 2024 at Olvera Street Plaza. It shows Aztec dancers beneath the statue of Spain's King Charles III, the monarch whose orders led to the founding of El Pueblo de la Reyna de Los Angles in 1781. Union Station, completed in 1939, appears in the background.

Her next step was to call on Harry Chandler, owner of the *Los Angeles Times* and arguably the most powerful man in Los Angeles of the 1920s. It was also around this time that she adopted the surname Sterling. Chandler liked her proposal to build a Mexican marketplace and likely saw the potential value in a popular tourist site for real estate worth in the LA area—something that would benefit him personally. He called one of his famous luncheons, and each guest chipped in $5,000 to create a for-profit organization with the mission to restore and recreate Olvera Street, with Sterling as the chief administrator. Sterling's project broke ground in 1929. The Los Angeles chief of police provided a labor force of twenty-five prisoners. Sterling wrote, "The prisoners were good workers. One escaped but we managed to keep the others." Sterling's dream, the revitalized Olvera Street, opened to the public on Easter Sunday 1930 and was an instant success. It remains a popular site for tourists, shoppers, and visitors to this day and is now one of the indispensable landmarks of downtown Los Angeles.

It would be nice to say that everything went smoothly for Christine Sterling after her tireless efforts led to the renaissance of Olvera Street and the commemorative plaza honoring the birth of Los Angeles. But that's not what happened. She lived in Chavez Ravine from 1938 to 1959 and was one of the residents evicted for the construction of Dodger Stadium. Afterward, she moved into the Avila Adobe (that she had successfully kept from demolition) and managed day-to-day operations of Olvera Street until her death in 1963 at the age of eighty-two.

Sterling's legacy is somewhat controversial. There are some who argue that her recreation of LA's Mexican past is just cultural appropriation and a Disneyland-like celebration of faux history. However, the buildings that stand to this day—besides the Avila Adobe, there's the hotel built by Pío Pico, the first firehouse, and the first Catholic church, which were all constructed at various points in the 1800s—are undeniably part of real history. And they all survive today because of the vision and tenacity of Christine Sterling. Writer Mike Schlitt quoted some of the people who live and work at Olvera Street today. "Mrs. Sterling was really a visionary" insists [shop owner] Mike Mariscal. "For her to just create this place and then to help poor Latino families to survive, that's what this place was born on." Mariscal's daughter, Christina Mariscal-Paten, a fifth-generation Olvera Street merchant, adds, "We are business owners, we are mom-and-pop shops, we . . . continue traditions."[6] California historian Kevin Starr summed up the legacy of Olvera Street: "Olvera Street might not be authentic Old California or even authentic Mexico, but it was better than the bulldozer."[7]

6   Mike Schlitt, "What's in a Street Name: Olvera Street Was Meant to Help Poor Latinos Survive," KCRW, April 4, 2022, www.kcrw.com/news/shows/greater-la/streets-ubi-insurrection/olvera-street-christine-sterling.

7   Nathan Masters, "A Brief History of the Los Angeles Plaza, the City's Misplaced Heart," PBS SoCal, February 1, 2012, www.pbssocal.org/shows/lost-la/a-brief-history-of-the-los-angeles-plaza-the-citys-misplaced-heart.

16

MUSIC, CULTURE, AND THE HOLLYWOOD BOWL

I was fortunate enough to be living in Hollywood, CA, when the underground punk rock music scene started. It was a small group of artists, misfits and weirdos

—Charlotte Caffey

ONE THING ABOUT working weekends as a rideshare driver is that you learn a lot about where people like to go when they go out: the popular clubs, bars, and concert venues. The closest major concert venue to where I live is the iconic Hollywood Bowl. Although I have dropped off and picked up concertgoers and sports fans all over the LA area, including places like the SoFi Stadium, the Forum, the

Walt Disney Concert Hall, the Staples Center, and Dodger Stadium, I've been to the Hollywood Bowl most often.

I remember picking up some folks after the last Tom Petty concert there (or anywhere) on September 25, 2017, only about a week before his tragic death from an accidental overdose. I recall talking with the fans who were there for his last concert of that year's tour, which turned out to be his last concert ever. They said that he still put on a great show. I told them about the time I went to his concert at the Forum in the late nineties. I related how he spoke to the audience in his signature Southern accent. "Hey," he said, "I know some of y'all are involved in the record industry, so I got a question to ask you." He paused, then continued. "Now you and I both know that it costs the same amount of money to manufacture a CD as it does to manufacture a cassette tape. So why do y'all have to charge more money for a CD?" The crowd erupted in cheers and applause. One thing Petty fans appreciated about him was his integrity and tell-it-like-it-is kind of honesty.

Another time, I picked up three women who had just attended a Dolly Parton concert at the Hollywood Bowl. As they were talking about the show, they also spoke about how much they admired her as a person. They described how she had donated millions of dollars to help many different people in need, including hurricane victims and children in poverty-stricken areas. One of them said, "I don't usually have much interest in listening to people talk about religion, especially if they're making a lot of money off it, like televangelists, but I actually didn't mind it when Dolly spoke about her faith."

"I know," said her friend. "She's so sincere, and you can tell she really believes in what she's saying. If I ever was going to let somebody preach to me, it would be her, not the 'professional' religious people."

Then there was the time I picked up two women on their way to a Duran Duran concert at the Bowl. Once they got in the car and I knew their destination, I asked them who was playing. After they mentioned it was the eighties group Duran Duran, I decided to play one of their songs, "Please Tell Me Now," that was featured on my Spotify list called Semi-Obscure 80s Songs. They asked me about the list. I told them it was a group of songs that were popular in the eighties, but they're almost never heard on totally eighties–type programs on classic rock stations. It has songs that were one-hit wonders like "Fanatic" by Felony, "Favourite Shirts" by Haircut 100, and "Turning Japanese" by the Vapors; it also has songs by artists who were better known but who are hardly ever played on classic rock stations, such as Blondie's "Touched by Your Presence" and "Cool Places" by Sparks and Jane Wiedlin of the Go-Gos.

"There was so much great music in the eighties," said one of them.

"I remember the best concert of my life," I said. "It was the Live Aid show at Wembley Stadium in London in the summer of 1985."

"You were there?" they asked.

"Yeah, I was," I said. "I was doing some volunteer work in London that summer, after my first year of college. My mom was a travel agent, so I asked her to help me figure out how to visit England on a budget. The solution was to do volunteer work. I didn't have to pay for my room or board, in exchange for working during the day, Monday through Friday, and so I had the evenings and weekends off to go to concerts or plays or do some sightseeing."

"And you got into the Live Aid concert?"

"Yeah. Well, I heard that two groups I really liked were going to be performing, the Who and Queen, and so I took the tube to Wembley Stadium and scalped a ticket for forty British pounds [at the time, that was about sixty American dollars] and then followed the crowd into the stadium. I actually managed to push my way up to the area between the stage and the tech tent that was about thirty yards from the stage."

"That must have been quite an experience."

"It definitely was," I said. "I saw just about anybody who was anybody in pop music in the early eighties, like Sting, Phil Collins, Dire Straits, David Bowie, Sade, and a bunch of other groups that were popular at that time. The concert was coordinated by Bob Geldof of the Boomtown Rats, and I think Pete Townshend of the Who helped put it together, too. I remember when I told my teenage daughter I was there; it sort of made me a hero in her eyes. I guess that concert has become something of an iconic event that's still talked about today. It was portrayed in the movie about Queen [*Bohemian Rhapsody*] at the very end of the film. It was like the last great appearance of Queen before their lead singer contracted AIDS, which led to his tragic death six years later." (The band did some live performances in 1986 but none that are as famous and iconic as the Live Aid concert in 1985.)

As we were talking, the song "Cool Places" came on. "That's Sparks with Jane Wiedlin of the Go-Gos."

One of the women said, "I love the Go-Gos! They were one of the greatest LA groups of the eighties." Just then, we pulled up to the drop-off area near the Bowl. "I think it was here where I saw them."

"I saw them at the Greek Theatre," I said.

"Oh, that's right," she said. "It was at the Greek."

"I remember something that happened during the concert that I never forgot, maybe because it showed a bit of the personality of Belinda Carlisle. Some guy from the audience jumped up onstage in front of her and grabbed a pair of underwear from his pants and started waving it in front of her face while she was singing, and she just kept on singing, acting as if he wasn't there. Meanwhile, two security guys in black shirts rushed at the guy simultaneously from both sides of the stage. They grabbed him and threw him down and started punching him."

The women weren't happy about this. "Why did they have to do that?"

"I guess the fact that she was a woman made the security guys feel like they had to be really protective of her," I said.

"Yes, that's possible," one of the women said.

"When Belinda saw them start pounding the guy, she broke character for the first time and said, 'Oh, don't hurt him!' It was kind of a cool moment because she completely ignored the guy while he was dancing in front of her, but when he got taken down, she stopped in the middle of the song and told the bouncers to take it easy."

"The Go-Gos were a great band."

"Yeah," I agreed, "they were one of the two really good all-girl rock bands to emerge from the LA scene during the eighties. The other group was the Bangles."

"I wasn't much of a Bangles fan," one of the women said.

"Me, either," said her companion. "But I guess you liked them, huh?"

"Yeah," I admitted. "Maybe it was a guy thing. I mean, Susanna Hoffs had those killer eyes and that pretty face, you know? And they had a couple of songs that were really good, like 'Manic Monday' and 'Walk Like an Egyptian.' Remember those?"

"Yeah, but I just didn't like them as much as everyone else."

"I had a chance to see them before they were really big, but I blew it."

"What do you mean?"

"They were playing at a club in the early eighties, and they weren't really famous yet, so it wasn't a very big club. But it was on Sunset Strip, so maybe they were starting to get somewhere. I had gone into the club with my brother and my friend Karl, and we were going to see them perform. But I didn't like the opening act, which was a group called Rain Parade, and I was feeling kind of tired, so I walked back to the car and went to sleep. Later the Bangles came on and my brother and friend told me about their performance, and I was sorry I left before they took the stage. I never ended up seeing them in concert, even though I bought a couple of their albums and listened to their music a lot of times."

The women told me about a group that was playing the clubs in the early eighties and asked if I had heard of them. I told them the name sounded familiar, but I wasn't sure. One of them said, "That was my brother's band." I remember seeing some groups that were somewhat famous in the eighties club scene of LA but that never achieved the kind of lasting fame of groups like Van Halen, Guns and Roses, and the Go-Gos. I told them how I remembered club concerts by groups like Felony, the Blasters, and the Jim Carroll Band. I especially remembered how Jim Carroll performed in a black raincoat for the whole concert, even though it was a warm summer evening.

"They made a movie about him," one of the women said.

"Who? Jim Carroll?"

"Yeah. Leonardo DiCaprio played him. It came out in the nineties."

"That's right," her friend replied. "It was called *Basketball Diaries*. That was such a sad movie."

"Well," I replied, "I think Jim Carroll had a sad and difficult life. But I guess like a lot of other creative artists, all the suffering he experienced and everything he went through helped contribute to his art."

"I suppose you're right," one of the women said. "Maybe if they didn't suffer so much, they wouldn't be able to produce the things they do."

"I once quoted a line about that from the Steve Miller Band song 'Jet Airliner' in a philosophy class—essentially, you have to go through Hades before you get to Valhalla."

17

THE COVID-19 PANDEMIC AND ALBERT CAMUS

In the depth of winter I finally learned that there was in me an invincible summer.

—Albert Camus

FOR A FEW weeks of March and early April 2020, everything in the city of Los Angeles (and probably all big cities) shut down. There was a dramatic drop in demand for Lyft rides, since there were a lot fewer places available to go out to. I remember the strange, bittersweet phenomenon of almost-empty freeways and streets. Suddenly, it became easier and faster to get around because there was so little traffic, but there was a sort of heaviness about it, because I knew that people were losing their businesses and jobs. The types of people who were passengers also changed somewhat. There were far fewer people going out to restaurants, bars, and clubs, but it seemed like a greater number of passengers were nurses, grocery store workers, and cooks at places that did a brisk take-out business. Meanwhile, restaurants that could not adapt closed their doors for good. I was sorry to see places like Souplantation, Hometown Buffet, and Fuddrucker's go out of business, never to return.

My day job also underwent drastic changes, as all of my classes started meeting remotely by Zoom. Although I was grateful to still have my job, I found this time to be extremely frustrating. At first, it was the sense that I had not been adequately trained to teach online, combined with the daily struggle to figure out how to do it. Then, after I more or less got the hang of it, there was the realization that most of my students were not really learning much because they were still teenagers and high school students, and the vast majority of people in those groups (other than a very small percentage of highly motivated superachievers) will not do much work if they are not accountable to a real teacher in the room with them. I began to realize that, even though I was able to retain my employment, I wasn't able to really educate the students who were showing up online but who were rarely responding immediately when I called on them. It became painfully obvious what was happening during the two- or three-second delay between when I called a student's name and they responded, "Oh, did you just call on me?" I'm almost certain they were gaming, listening to music, texting their friends, or on Instagram. Because we weren't allowed to require students to be on camera, they were doing other things. Thus, I ended each day with a sense of frustration and ineffectiveness.

It was during those months of 2020 and the spring of 2021 that I found Lyft driving to be a welcome escape from the computer and the sense of educational impotence that fell upon me each day.

Instead of spending seemingly endless hours in front of a computer trying to teach students who weren't really responding, I could get out into the world and take people where they needed to go and feel like I was really helping people. Even though many restaurants, bars, and other businesses were shut down, transportation, just like grocery stores and hospitals, was always considered a necessary industry, so Uber and Lyft continued to operate, albeit with new requirements for mask-wearing and no more than one passenger (or couple, or small group) at a time.

As I mentioned, for the first few weeks of the shutdown (starting in March 2020), there was a sharp drop in demand, but things gradually started to pick up again. Eventually, businesses reopened, albeit with mask mandates, and the regular patterns of work and traffic returned.

During that time I wrote a book review that certain friends (including some who are actually French) have enjoyed a great deal. I was waiting in line at a local Costco because, at that time, that was what one had to do to be able to buy a big package of toilet paper, and I was reading *La Peste (The Plague)* by Albert Camus. It was one of those books I had been meaning to read for years, and the pandemic seemed about the best time to do it. As I waited for hours in line, I did a significant amount of reading, which led to a thoughtful posting on my Facebook page, which caught the attention of my stepmother (Elaine Madsen), who edits an online magazine of arts and culture (Felix.co), and she asked me to write a full review of the novel by Camus, which I did. Because I have sometimes discussed Camus novels and philosophy with Lyft passengers, the review is included here. This is reprinted as it appeared in *Felix* magazine, with the permission of the editor.

A Novel for Our (Pandemic) Times: *The Plague*, by Albert Camus

In the throes of the Covid Pandemic, we may feel that we are the first ones to confront a situation in which life seems absurd, indecision and boredom abound, and uncertainty about how to act leads to paralysis of the will. But we would be wrong. The generation that emerged from all the horrors and destruction of World War II, and the Great Depression that preceded it, confronted a reality whose challenges exceeded—or at least paralleled—our own. Jean Paul Sartre and the philosophy of existentialism are perhaps the dominant cultural/intellectual phenomena of post-war Europe. But the writer who, I believe, speaks more powerfully to our own times was neither an existentialist (though he is often classified as such, unjustly), nor a close ally of Sartre, though he was, for a time, his good friend. Perhaps it is too crude a summary to say that Albert Camus retained his idealism, while Sartre basically "sold out." But it is not that different from what Sartre himself wrote upon hearing of the tragic death of Camus in a car accident on Jan. 4, 1960: "His obstinate humanism, narrow and pure . . . waged an uncertain war against the massive and formless events of the time."

Perhaps one of the best uses of our "indoor" time during a pandemic is to take a look—or another look—at a work of fiction that conveys an obstinate humanism that wages a sort of war on the absurdity of our situation, without falling into despair or inactivity. That work is *The Plague*, by Albert Camus, which was first published in 1948: the same year that George Orwell finished *1984*. Though Orwell and Camus never met, they traveled similar intellectual paths. Both of them witnessed the suffering and oppression of the lower classes, and for a time flirted with Marxism/socialism as a means for improving the lot of the suffering poor. However, they both reached a point where they realized that the Marxist philosophy that promised to improve the lives of the poor and oppressed, in fact led to the Soviet gulags of Josef Stalin. So Orwell wrote *Animal*

Farm, and Camus had a very public falling out with Sartre, who had become an apologist for Stalin's brutal oppression. Camus was more of an "outsider" in his own time, and so he perhaps did not have as big of a stature among the fashionable intellectuals and nihilists of the Paris cafés of the 1950s. But his unflinching moral idealism, in the face of tremendous suffering and apparent absurdity, is, I would argue, what makes him a more compelling thinker for our times. Can we still care, can we act, can we still retain our humanity in the face of a worldwide pandemic? *The Plague* may not have all the answers, but it can light an intellectual path by which we might find some—if not all—the answers we seek.

The first chapters describe how the plague comes upon the city. At first people have no idea of the seriousness of the disease; they simply begin to find an unusual number of dead rats throughout their neighborhoods. There are passages that bear an uncanny resemblance to the Covid pandemic of 2020. Of course there are some clear differences as well: the story of Camus is set within the confines of the city of Oran (in then French North Africa, currently the independent nation of Algeria). In the novel, the plague is an outbreak of bubonic plague which spreads from rats to humans. But the progression among the people in the novel from disbelief to surprise, then panic is eerily prescient of our own time. The confusion and uncertainty of the city officials in the novel mirrors the uncertainty and confusion caused in many countries during the Covid Pandemic of 2020. There are debates about how to respond, how to proceed without causing general panic among the people, and, later in the story, how to deal with overcrowded emergency wards, and grisly discussions of what to do with the overwhelming number of corpses.

In the amazingly perceptive dystopian scenario created by Camus, the author describes the economic shutdown in the city of Oran: "While our townspeople were trying to come to terms with their sudden isolation, the plague was posting sentries at the gates and turning away ships bound for Oran . . . The commercial activity that hitherto made it one of the chief ports on the coast had ceased abruptly." He also describes how some of the local shops and businesses are boarded up, some never to reopen. Another passage that seems a prophetic anticipation of the pandemic of 2020 describes how the city's funerals undergo change: "The plague victim died away from his family and the customary vigil beside the dead body was forbidden . . . needless to say, the family was notified, but in most cases, since the deceased had lived with them, its members were in quarantine and thus immobilized."

But *The Plague* is a compelling read, not simply because it accurately predicts several aspects of our current reality from the desk of a writer working in the late 1940s; but because it also compels its readers—at least those who take its implications to heart—from indifference and inaction to involvement and benevolent action. Or to put it in today's "street language" it takes the position of: "I don't give a crap about anyone else" and argues with it, to force the realization: "No, I do care. And I will get involved." The most powerful presentation of this theme in the novel is in Part Four (there are five parts). The journalist Rambert, who was not a regular resident of the town, found himself "trapped" in it because of the plague, when no one was allowed in or out. To fill the time, he begins helping Dr. Rieux, who, like the other doctors of the city, is overwhelmed with the numbers of sick and dying patients. Rambert is also quietly making arrangements with some shady smugglers to sneak out of the quarantined city, to get back to his beloved wife in Paris. After he has made all the arrangements, he suddenly decides to stay and continue helping Dr. Rieux to care for the plague victims. "Until now, I always felt a stranger in this town," Rambert reasons, "and that I'd no concern with you people. But now that I've seen what I've seen, I know that I belong here whether I want it or not. This business is everybody's business." When the doctor does not immediately reply, Rambert seems to grow annoyed: "But you know as well as I do, damn it! Or else what are you up to in that hospital of yours?" Not long afterward he says: "For nothing in the world is it worth turning one's back on what one loves. Yet that is what I am doing, though why I do not know."

What is so powerful and compelling about the change in Rambert is that it resonates with that moment in reality when apathy and inaction change into involvement for what is right. It's not the obvious conflict between good and evil present in so many other films and novels; it's the inner conflict between a character's preliminary indifference, changing into commitment to making a difference. It's what makes the classic film *Casablanca* (which, interestingly enough, is also set in French North Africa) one of the greatest pieces of cinematic art. Rick Blaine (Humphrey Bogart) goes from "I stick my neck out for nobody" to involvement and action against the Nazis, and the hero of the resistance, Viktor Lazlo ends up telling him: "Welcome to the fight." Other examples from cinema (based on actual people) are Oskar Schindler in *Schindler's List* and Paul Rusesabagina in *Hotel Rwanda*. They both decide, from a starting point of indifference, and at great personal risk, to get involved in saving innocent lives in the hundreds.

Finally, *The Plague* is a great read because it demonstrates how Camus becomes greater than existentialism. Existentialism focuses on the absurdity of life, and responds with uncertainty and moral paralysis. By contrast, Camus faces suffering and death, and the apparent absurdity of the human condition "head-on" but he does not excuse himself, or his audience from daring to care and get involved. This is clear in *The Plague*, and it is also powerfully stated in his Nobel Prize Acceptance Speech of 1957. "The writer's role," he stated, "is not free from difficult duties. By definition, he cannot put himself today at the service of those who make history; he is at the service of those who suffer it . . . Not all the armies of tyranny with their millions of men will free him from this isolation, even and particularly if he falls into step with them. But the silence of an unknown prisoner, abandoned to humiliations at the other end of the world, is enough to draw the writer out of his exile, at least whenever, in the midst of the privileges of freedom, he manages not to forget that silence, and to transmit it in order to make it resound by means of his art." That is not the language of one who, when confronted with the absurdity of life, refuses to act. Later in the speech, he defines the obligations of a writer in greater detail:

> But in all circumstances of life, in obscurity or temporary fame, cast in the irons of tyranny or for a time free to express himself, the writer can win the heart of a living community that will justify him, on the condition that he will accept to the limit of his abilities the two tasks that constitute the greatness of his craft: the service of truth and the service of liberty. Because his task is to unite the greatest possible number of people, his art must not compromise with lies and servitude . . . Whatever our personal weaknesses may be, the nobility of our craft will always be rooted in two commitments, difficult to maintain: the refusal to lie about what one knows and the resistance to oppression.

At the conclusion of his speech, he does not simply thank the Nobel Academy for the honor they bestowed on him. He states that he "would receive it as an homage rendered to all those who, sharing in the same fight, have not received any privilege, but have on the contrary known misery and persecution." Like Rambert in *The Plague*, Camus chooses to recognize and serve those less fortunate, who are suffering and unsung when he could easily ignore them and live in ease and comfort. And so his novel, like his other works, challenges us to face the absurdity, suffering and death around us, and to react not with apathy and moral paralysis, but with action: in service to truth and freedom, and our suffering fellow travelers. *The Plague* speaks to us now, and will continue to do so for future generations, as long as there is humanity, with all its suffering, ambiguity, and absurdity.

*   *   *

Lastly, a few thoughts that were in my original posting on Facebook about Camus's book that would later lead to the book review that was published in *Felix* magazine. I decided to cut these lines because I wasn't sure if the discussion of religion fit for the audience of the online magazine. However, they do add a deeper perspective to the discussion, and so they are included here:

> Religion, I think, can give us reasons why, but for thinkers like Camus, who cannot derive the benefit of religious belief, his philosophy provides the next best thing: to do what is right, even if you cannot explain why. One of the statements Christ made when he was questioned before Pilate was this: "Anyone who is committed to the truth hears my voice" (Jn. 18:37). I like to think that he had people like Albert Camus (and my father) in mind: people who may not believe in God but who commit themselves to the truth as they perceive it and thereby do God's work on earth, even if they may not know it or may not be able to explain why.

18

THE WHITE BOY GANGSTA AND TATTOOS ON THE HEART

The highest religious and spiritual ideals of any faith would invite us to a compassion for all lives destroyed by the violence that plagues us.

—Father Greg Boyle, SJ

SOME OF THE most interesting passengers are people with criminal pasts. One young man mentioned how he had been making millions of dollars at the age of nineteen by dealing narcotics. He managed to avoid being arrested for a long time (months, maybe even a few years) by enrolling as a college student and being extremely careful about whom he trusted. He told me that he knew the feds were after him, but he managed to play the game and get other people to make his drops without revealing his real identity for a long time. At some point, he heard about people he trusted who had been arrested, and he realized that it was likely only a matter of time before someone got to him. Sure enough, somebody who had been arrested decided to snitch on him, and some agents showed up at his apartment and took him in. I asked him, "Were they FBI or DEA agents?"

He replied, "Yeah." I guess he meant that they were both or else he didn't know. What happened to him? He spent a few years in jail, then was paroled on good behavior. He decided to move west to Southern California and make a new life for himself, this time with a straight job and no more narcotics dealing. He said, "They're watching me now, and I have to fly right." I asked him how it was going, and he indicated that he was doing well, but sometimes he missed the excitement of his bad days. I told him that if he ever decides to write about his experiences, he has a lot of stories he could use. "Oh yeah!" he exclaimed. "I'm going to write a book about it someday." Not long after he said that, we reached his destination, and it was time to say farewell.

Another passenger was a friendly young man who was covered in tattoos. When I met him, he had recently gotten out of jail and was going to visit his parents. I'm not sure why he had done time, but it was definitely related to gang activity. He said, "I know it's funny, because I'm a white boy, and you don't see a lot of white boys who are gangstas, but I was one of them. I mean, sometimes they made fun of me, but I was just as much a gangsta as any of them."

"But since you got out of jail, you haven't gone back?"

"No, man. I'm all clean now. I don't do any of that gang shit anymore. Now I'm devoted to my Lord and savior, Jesus Christ. That's who I am now."

"That's good," I said. "Was there someone or something that influenced you to make that change in your life?"

"Yeah, there was," he said. "My homeboy, G."

"G?"

"Yeah, Father Greg," he said. "That dude's legit, man. He influenced me to find God and give up being a gangsta. You heard of him?"

"Yeah, I heard of him," I said. "He started Homeboy Industries to help former gang members work and build up their lives once they decide to quit the gangsta lifestyle."

"That's him!" he replied excitedly. "Man, that dude is the real deal. He really cared about me and helped me turn my life around, and he does that for a lot of us."

"Is there a book I can read if I want to find out more about him?"

"Yeah, his book came out some years ago. It's called *Tattoos on the Heart*."

"All right," I said. "I'll check it out." A lot of people say something like that and never end up doing it, but I did get on Amazon and order a copy of it.

Over the next few weeks and months, I read *Tattoos on the Heart* and was very impressed by Father Boyle and his work to bring God's love and peace to young people whose lives had been ravaged by hatred, violence, and killing. He explains the title in the preface:

> Once, after dealing with a particularly exasperating homie named Sharkey, I switch my strategy and decide to catch him in the act of doing the right thing . . . I tell him how heroic he is and how the courage he now exhibits in transforming his life far surpasses the hollow "bravery" of his barrio past. I tell him he is a giant among men. I mean it. Sharkey seems thrown off balance by all this and silently stares at me. Then he says, "Damn, G . . . I'm gonna tattoo that on my heart."[8]

---

8   Gregory Boyle, *Tattoos on the Heart: The Power of Boundless Compassion* (New York: Free Press, 2011), xiv.

In the introduction, Father Boyle describes how he started work at Dolores Mission, "the poorest parish in the Archdiocese of Los Angeles,"[9] in 1984 and became its pastor in 1986. "I buried my first young person killed because of gang violence in 1988, and as of this writing, I have been called upon for this sad task an additional 167 times."[10] Throughout the remaining pages, the author describes many of the young people he got to know and help, some of whom would end up getting gunned down, others, like the young man who was my passenger, who succeeded in rebuilding their lives after growing up and out of the gangsta lifestyle on the mean streets of LA.

I first heard of Dolores Mission in the summer of 1989 when I stayed with the Catholic Worker Community as a volunteer intern for two months and helped to feed the homeless at their soup kitchen on Skid Row. (It's called a soup kitchen, but it actually provides full meals to hundreds of homeless people.) One of the community leaders told me about Dolores Mission: "That's our parish." At the time, I was part of the choir at a church in El Segundo (Saint Andrew's Russian Greek Catholic Church), so I never attended Dolores Mission on Sundays, but I would hear about it and Father Boyle many times in the years to come.

---

9   Boyle, *Tattoos* on the Heart, 1.
10   Boyle, *Tattoos* on the Heart, 2.

This is a picture of Dolores Mission taken December 23, 2022, with the skyscrapers of downtown LA visible in the background. It seems quiet and peaceful, but it has been the center of tremendous tragedy and inspiration.

After my internship with the Catholic Worker, I started teaching high school in the 1990s. I read about Father Boyle and Homeboy Industries, but I was busy with my teaching career and fatherhood when that entered the picture in 1997, the year my firstborn child began her life in the womb of Mrs. Carstens. So I never actually read Father Boyle's book until my passenger recommended it to me. I was very impressed by Father Boyle and his description of the work he does with the troubled youth of LA. Although I can't say I agree with all he has said (let's just say I agree with Pope John Paul II and Benedict XVI on certain controversial and unpopular teachings of the Catholic Church), I have nothing but respect for the way in which he has turned so many gangstas around and helped them find Christ.

Not long after I read *Tattoos on the Heart*, I recommended it to my youngest daughter, who was also, at the time, a student in my college class. After she said that she enjoyed it, I told her she could write a review of it for one of the essays that was required in the class she was taking (from one of the most popular instructors at College of the Canyons—her old man!). She wrote a fine review, and so it follows next.

*   *   *

A Review of *Tattoos on the Heart* by Catherine Carstens

When traversing the city of Los Angeles in search of the nearest Starbucks or Insta-worthy photo opportunity, there are always those parts that cause the average tourist to lock their doors, speed up a little if driving, or clutch their purses a little closer and quicken their pace if on foot, averting their eyes in either scenario. Behind all of the star-studded neighborhoods, beautiful beaches, ostentatious mansions, and high-end shopping malls that draw millions of tourists to Los Angeles each year, there lies the reality of the dirty underbelly of the city: tens of thousands of people struggling through homelessness, violent gang activity, unemployment, poverty, or sometimes a mix of all these. The poorer neighborhoods that contain the aforementioned populations often remain ignored or forgotten by those who are more fortunate, swept under the rug and given only a passing thought, like an unpleasant smell one wishes to escape. These are the "bad parts" of the City of Angels; the parts nobody likes to acknowledge. However, just as there are many who immerse themselves only in the shiny exterior of this city, there are a select few who choose to focus their efforts on finding beauty within its ugliness.

When we consider these few, perhaps there are no better works to discuss than *Tattoos on the Heart*, a book containing a collection of memoirs written by Father Gregory Boyle relating to his charity work and experiences as a priest at Dolores Mission, the poorest church in the Catholic Archdiocese of Los Angeles. Rather than averting their eyes when faced with the lost or broken-spirited,

Father Boyle encourages readers to look even deeper into their stories and inevitably discover the humanity that irrevocably ties them together. By recounting the ways in which he was able to bring hope and love to the loveless and hopeless, Father Boyle proves over and over that everyone is deserving of compassion and that there is no such thing as a lost cause in the eyes of God.

What I found to be most striking in Father Boyle's narrative was his encounters with failure and loss over and over again. Father Boyle described almost as many tales of defeat as he did of triumph. He wrote about being too familiar with the funerals of homeboys he knew since childhood, relapses from those he had given jobs and money to, hospital visits to those who had become victim to gang violence, and the unmistakable cries of grieving mothers. He encountered absolutely gut-wrenching scenes of death, absolute misery, and terror, and throughout it all, he never wavered from his faith in God. If one story could perfectly sum up the attitude with which Father Boyle approached his work, it would be the time when he described being ecstatically visited by one of the children who frequented his parish in the middle of an important meeting to present him with a report card that displayed all Fs. Father Boyle inspected the report card and praised the boy for the one positive aspect he could find: zero absences. His unconditional love for and support of those who were not used to receiving it caused a real difference in the lives of all he interacted with, even the ones who went back to their lives of crime or ended up dead due to the path they were on. They were able to experience unending compassion thanks to the church and the work of Father Boyle. He attributes his mindset toward failure to this quote from Mother Teresa: "God does not call us to be successful, but only to be faithful."

The topic of criminal reform is an extremely divisive and polarizing one, especially in the modern political climate of contention regarding issues like the death penalty and leniency relating to violent criminals. One might mistake *Tattoos on the Heart* for erring on the side of being too forgiving to those members of society who are undeserving of second chances. However, I would argue that the idea of Christlike forgiveness cannot be equated with allowing the evil and wicked to be welcomed back into society without due consequence to their crimes. Rather, it gives the push to those who need it to return themselves to a life that is good and full of love rather than hatred. It begs them to change their inner values and return to a state of purity once they have strayed. It is not about mindlessly forgiving people simply because they ask for it. It is about being the one who keeps the door open for those who want to come back into the light.

Additionally, Father Boyle's work emphasizes how the urge to separate oneself from the marginalized should be rejected. It is all too common for people to disregard those in need of help in order to maintain their own comfort. People like to care from a safe distance and keep the bad and scary things at an arm's length from themselves. Concerning this matter, he wrote about how the parish in which he works had begun to smell faintly from the hundreds of homeless people who took shelter in the church at night, leading to several complaints and an eventual meeting regarding the matter of hygiene. In response to the situation, Father Boyle reminds them why the church smells the way it does, leading the parishioners to conclude that the church does not just smell like feet; it smells like their commitment to doing what Jesus would do. As Father Boyle writes about healing the ill, "They're ripping the roof off the place, and those outside are being let in." He takes the people for what they are: the good, the bad, and the downright smelly. No separation could be found from himself and those whom he helped: he assimilated their culture, spoke their language, ate their food, learned their ways, and used his knowledge to help them from the inside out. At no point did he consider himself above those he was helping or deserving of any better than they were despite the differences in their lives. He was able to prove that the differences between the average person and these gang members were due only to life circumstances and that, at the core, everyone is the same. Even in the cases of orchestrating peace treaties between enemy gangs or introducing them to each other before becoming coworkers, Father Boyle did not allow the "otherness" created by this environment to permeate the spaces he controlled. After witnessing several reconciliations between sworn enemies, he went so far as to remark that it is impossible to hate who you know. This same logic applies to those who would rather turn away than extend a hand to those in need out of a false sense of superiority due to social class or any other unimportant detail. If only one really knew these people, it would be impossible to maintain such an attitude. This book bridges that gap by bringing the stories of countless gang members to anyone who is willing to pick it up. Like Father Boyle said, it is impossible to hate who one knows, and once one reads *Tattoos on the Heart*, a person truly does know the lives, hearts, and stories of those who fill these pages.

It would be remiss to write a review about this book without mentioning the most important part of it: the people whose stories it chronicles. Father Boyle's book focuses mainly on the gang members he attempted to get out of their dangerous lifestyle by giving them legitimate jobs and a chance to start over. Even while in jail, on the streets, or facing a life with no future, these former gangbangers still found it within themselves to give peace a chance. When faced with an abusive childhood, no parental support, minimal education, and no positive role models, it can only be too easy to fall into the life of violence and drugs that seems to dominate those around oneself. It is exceedingly difficult to make the decision to attempt to rise above those circumstances and give peace and love a chance. The indomitable human spirit is showcased over and over again by these men, women, and children who cling to the church and the life raft it provides to save them from themselves. Homeboy Industries, the organization started by Father Boyle, is an additional life raft for these people who are attempting to climb their way out of poverty. Through this organization, they are provided with legitimate jobs, offered social connections, anger management and parenting classes, free tattoo removal, and rehabilitation programs. It takes a lot of courage to ask for help, and these people's stories truly inspire any reader to possess even a fraction of that bravery. The ability to wash off the dirt, grime, and scars one has been given by life and still face the day with an inner purity and goodness that cannot be taken away by any beating down is truly extraordinary. This kind of trait cannot be taught, only uncovered. It is mysterious, nameless, inexplicable, and profound all at once.

The final thought I would like to end with about *Tattoos on the Heart* is this: These people may have been lost in the eyes of the world, but they were never lost in the eyes of God. People want to be good; they just need to be given the chance. Father Boyle shows how he gives them that chance throughout his decades devoted to helping those in need. His book is truly a read like no other and powerfully demonstrates the saving power of God's infinite love. His detractors may argue that his efforts are in vain, but Father Boyle proves that no attempt to do good will ever be a waste of time. This demonstration of commitment inspires readers to find their own ways to touch the lives of others around them in similar ways.

19

WHEN LA BURNED: THE FIRESTORM OF JANUARY, 2025

Though nothing can bring back the hour
Of splendour in the grass, of glory in the flower;
We will grieve not, rather find
Strength in what remains behind;
In the primal sympathy
Which having been must ever be
In the soothing thoughts that spring
Out of human suffering;
In the faith that looks through death
In years the bring the philosophic mind

—William Wordsworth

Every year there are wildfires in California. During the luckier years, they burn in the wilderness areas, and few or no homes or businesses are lost. However, in January of 2025, the dry and windy conditions combined in such a way that the biggest and most destructive fires happened, not only in the history of California, but in the history of the United States. The sheer number of acres scorched, homes burnt and property lost surpassed those of any other fires at any time up to this point. As of this writing, some of the fires are still burning, but there is some measure of containment, and firefighters from all over the country —and even some from other countries—are working to halt their paths of destruction.

The whole world watched as an astounding number of homes and businesses, including world-famous celebrities' homes in some of the nicest areas of Pacific Palisades and Malibu were lost. We watched as the homes of Dick Van Dyke, Mel Gibson, Paris Hilton, Lady Gaga, James Woods and many others, including a large number in Altadena, as well as some in Sylmar and Hollywood Hills were burnt to the ground. I received text messages of concern and support from friends in France and Florida.

While all of this was happening, I still worked as a teacher and a Lyft driver. One lady I spoke with was convinced that the fires were the result of a conspiracy. I wasn't sure if I agreed with her, but she did mention some interesting facts. We'll call her Mabel. She was a black lady, and she mentioned the fires that were set on purpose by a white racist mob in Tulsa, Oklahoma, in 1921. The area known as Black Wall Street was one of the wealthiest black communities in the country, and it was devastated after 35 blocks were destroyed in the fires. "They doin' the same thing now," Mabel said. "They moving people off so they can get their land!" She described how insurance companies cancelled policies for many homes only months before the fires, and also how reservoirs didn't have enough water. I told her that I had read about how Altadena was a sort of "mecca" for successful black families since the 50s and 60s. "That's right," she said, "that's what they doing, just like they did in Tulsa in 1921!" I told her that if anyone did this on purpose, I sure hope they would get exposed and punished.

Mabel also mentioned the massive destruction in Maui, and how a lot of people showed up soon afterwards to offer to buy the land from the people who had lost their homes. "You watch," she told me, "after these fires are done, a bunch of speculators are gonna come out and try to buy up everyone's homes!" I told her that it might be like that, or it might just be a lack of good planning on the part of the city and state officials. Soon after that, it was time to drop her off.

Sometimes I wonder if she may be right? I also see comments from people online who speculate that all the destruction may be the wrath of God for all the sinful things that have come out of Hollywood. That's a possibility, of course, but for my part I think I prefer to let others discuss and debate the causes of the disaster. My own responses are to reflect, to pray and to act to help.

On January 17 (about ten days after the fires started), I posted this on my Facebook page, below the quote from Wordsworth that appears at the beginning of this chapter:

> I woke up this morning & got ready for work; I looked around at the walls and the lights of the home where I've lived since 2001. I asked myself what would I do if all of this were gone? I try to imagine what so many of my fellow "Angelos" are going through. What can I do for them? I'm not rich, I don't have a lot of spare time. I can donate to charity. I can try to volunteer, perhaps at a Red Cross facility. I can think of the victims and pray for them. I'm not sure what else. I suppose I can write my thoughts on FB; I can remind myself (and anyone else who reads it) that this is not our true and permanent home, and none of us really owns anything. One of my

favorite quotes from Ernest Hemingway is this: "A man can be destroyed but not defeated." That was in his novel, The Old Man and the Sea, in which an aging fisherman, through grit and determination, manages to catch the biggest marlin anyone has ever seen. Though he is no longer physically strong, his spirit is strong and unbreakable. So the quote above means that a real man does not give up, even in the face of overwhelming defeat. If I lost my house tomorrow (and there's no guarantee that can't happen, since not all the fires are out, and not all the dry, windy conditions are over), I hope I would still carry on, and fulfill my duties as a husband, father and teacher. Of course I would probably need to get some new clothes, but friends have been telling me that for years... I don't think the essence of who we are as human beings is or should be measured by the sum of what we possess.

While much of what we in LA possessed was lost, on a far more massive scale than any previous set of fires, I'm confident we will rebuild and we will be back. But LA will never be the same. Some things were lost which cannot be replaced. In addition to the vast numbers of private homes and businesses that were lost, one of the most tragic losses was the Will Rogers Residence, the historic home that used to occupy the center of the Will Rogers State Historic Park. This was part of the cultural legacy of Los Angeles, and unlike homes of current celebrities, it can never be rebuilt. But we can honor its memory.

Who was Will Rogers? For those who may not know, Will Rogers was about the most popular entertainer of the 1930s. He was born a citizen of the Cherokee Nation in 1879, and first achieved fame as a horseman and rope performer. Later he became a star in silent movies, wrote a regular newspaper column and became a beloved story-teller and commentator on radio. Some of his sayings are still quoted and posted up to the present day. "Even if you're on the right track," he once quipped, "you'll get run over if you just sit there." Another of his widely quoted sayings was this: "I am not a member of an organized political party. I am a Democrat." Referring to his Native American ancestry, he said: "My ancestors didn't come on the Mayflower, but they met the boat when it landed." There are hundreds of his quotes that can still be found online, but I'll include one more here, which is one of my favorites: "No man is great if he thinks he is."

At the height of his fame (in the 1920s), Rogers purchased 359 acres of land in Santa Monica (now Pacific Palisades) that became a 31-room house and guest quarters, and included a polo field, horse-racing facilities and a golf course. Rogers used to enjoy riding horses with family and friends to the beach and back, at a time (in the 1930s) when that area of Santa Monica was mostly open fields. The beach that used to be his riding destination is still named Will Rogers State Beach in his honor. While much of the land of his original spread is still there, including hiking trails and the polo field, unfortunately the residence was completely destroyed in the LA Firestorm of 2025.

This is a picture of the Will Rogers Residence, taken from the hiking trail behind the house, with the polo field and forested areas of the Will Rogers State Historic Park in the background.

This is the living room of the Will Rogers residence, where many famous film stars, literati and politicians of the 20s and 30s stayed when they came to visit. A park ranger can be seen on the left, and portraits of Will and his wife, Betty hang on the wall to the right. Some of these items were saved, but the structure is gone.

Although the residence is gone, the surrounding park is most likely still there. As of this writing, the area is still closed to the public, but the hiking trails and polo field may still have something of a future. The pictures on the next page show some of the surrounding area, as seen from the hiking trails behind the residence.

This is a picture of one of the hiking trails behind the Will Rogers Residence. The ocean is visible in the distance, though it may not show very well in this shot.

This is a picture of the view of some of the palatial homes from the hiking trail behind the Will Rogers Residence. None of the homes were there in the 1920s, and it's uncertain if any are still there in 2025.

Before I conclude this description of the time when LA burned in the Firestorm of 2025, I'd like to focus on some of the silver linings behind the dark clouds. Whenever there are stories of great catastrophes, there are stories of heroism, courage and self-sacrifice that go along with it. In the case of the firestorm, there are numerous stories of neighbors helping neighbors get to safety; one of the most poignant of these was told by the 99 year old actor, Dick Van Dyke. He described how he was crawling around in front of his house, and neighbors came up and helped him to join in the evacuation. "I don't think I would have made it..." he said, "So they saved my life..." There are many other stories that have been told of people who took in their friends or family members who lost their homes, who saved wandering pets, and who donated generously to help the victims. One story I heard on the radio mentioned how some restaurants (such as the iconic SoCal hamburger chain, In'n'Out) were serving free food for all firefighters who showed up in their restaurants. On the radio, one DJ described how a group of firefighters walked into a restaurant, and the whole place erupted in spontaneous clapping and cheering. It made sense considering how they risk their lives as part of their jobs, and how many of them came to Los Angeles from places far from So-Cal, including other states and countries.

As fortune would have it, during the time the firestorm was mostly, but not completely over, I gave a ride to a young fireman, along with his girlfriend and one of his buddies. He was off duty at the time, so at first I didn't know what he did for a living. He asked me about what I did, and I mentioned that, in addition to Lyft driving, my "day job" was as a high school English teacher. Not long after that, I found out he was a fireman, and said: "Well, thank you for your service. I guess in a time like this you guys are the heroes of the hour!"

"Yeah," he said, "it's been nice to get all the love we've been getting from the public!"

"So were you involved," I asked, "in fighting the Palisades Fire or the Eaton Fire? I think those were the two biggest."

"That's right," he said. "I didn't work on the Palisades Fire, but I was deployed to the Eaton Fire."

"Wow! I'm sure you saw some intense stuff!

"Yeah, but I didn't really think about it like that. I was just focused on doing my job and trying to help stop the fires we could get to."

"Well, I really appreciate all the work you and your coworkers did in the face of what must have seemed overwhelming conditions!"

"We were just doing our jobs."

"In fact, I don't know if I can change what's in the app, but I'd like to give you this ride free of charge."

"Don't worry about that!" he laughed. "It's not that big a deal, I can afford it. And you guys deserve to get paid, too! Heck, I'm grateful for what you do as a teacher! We need guys (and gals) like you to help kids learn. I'm sure your job can be tough as well!"

"Yeah, that's true," I agreed. "But at a time like this, it's people in your line of work who seem to be the most important. Is your fire station around here?"

"No, actually my station is in Bakersfield. But a bunch of us were sent down here to help out."

"I heard there's a lot firefighters from out of town who came here to help!"

"Oh, yeah," he said, "there's a lot of them from all kinds of places."

I remember I saw a firetruck that said: "Caldwell Fire Dept." and when I looked it up later after I got home, the only Caldwell I found was a small town in Idaho!"

"Well, our job is to help out where it's needed, and you guys in LA needed it."

"I sure appreciate you guys, and so do a lot of us Angelenos!"

He laughed and said, "Thanks, man, it's nice to be appreciated!"

After that ride was over, I remember thinking how there are many forms of public service that can be tough, require dedication and are worthy of thanks. A teacher thanked a firefighter and the firefighter thanked the teacher. When I see cops in donut shops or Starbucks, sometimes I thank them for their service, too. Anyone who puts themselves at risk to keep others safe has my deep respect. It took a firestorm for us to really appreciate the work of firefighters. But teachers, cops, air traffic controllers, medical personnel and transit workers all deserve our thanks as well. They also help lift LA, and every other city on the face of God's earth. As Dietrich Bonhoeffer once wrote: "In normal life we hardly realize how much more we receive than we give, and life cannot be right without such gratitude."

20
AFTERWORD

—William Shakespeare, *The Tempest*

THIS BOOK HAS grown over a period of several years, roughly between 2016 and 2024. I didn't know exactly the shape it would take, but after I decided to work on it, it gradually developed itself. It became a love letter to the people of the city of Los Angeles, a bridge between past and present, an amalgam of literature, history, philosophy, psychology, and theology. I wrote it for my passengers, my family and friends: for those who read books, and perhaps for those who don't read books but might find it worthwhile to read *this* one. It's the distilled concoction that gets created when a nerdy bookworm and English teacher hits the streets of the big city and listens to all sorts of different people who inhabit it.

Back in 1986, I was a student (in my early 20s) studying in Cambridge, England. We had a number of distinguished guest speakers who came and spoke to our group. Two of the most well-known were Howard Fast and Maeve Binchy. One piece of advice from Ms. Binchy that I never forgot was that if you seek to be a good writer, "Use your eye as a camera and use your ear as a tape recorder." I never forgot her advice, and this book has been my attempt to apply it to the experiences I've had as a rideshare driver, combined with my experiences as a teacher of local history.

And so I thank you for reading this. If it has brought you some enjoyment, learning, insight, or laughter, it has achieved its task. I am also grateful to all the people who have been my passengers, who have shared with me a small part (or sometimes more than that) of the essence of who they are. I have listened to celebrities and ordinary unknown people, long-time residents of LA and visiting tourists or recent immigrants, young people struggling with relationships, and older people talking about their life and times. Each of them has enriched me, and through this book, I hope they may have enriched you as well.

Finally, I am grateful to God for all of the people I've been privileged to meet, for my ability to write about them, for the beauty of the greater Los Angeles area, and for you and all the people who may someday read this book. It has been a blast. I've had my share of suffering and privations, but rideshare driving, teaching about local history, and writing about these things has been a joy and a privilege.

So I thank you, and if you have thoughts to share with me, I would invite you to contact me via this email address: *lyftinglawriter@ gmail.com.* My sincere thanks go to you, all who read this book, all who inspired it, all who helped me work on it, and to God. Deo gratias and ad majorem Dei gloriam.

INDEX OF PEOPLE IN LYFTING LA

INDEX OF PLACES IN LYFTING LA